The Flight

By

Jim Foreman

The Flight

The story of one man's
love affair with the
Piper Cub aircraft.

by

Jim Foreman

Contents

Foreword   7

Flight through History   11

The Flight   25

Following My Dream   179

FOREWORD

Perhaps, dear reader, you are one of the 325,000 graduates of the wartime Civilian Pilot Training Program of World War II who took your first flight training in the Piper Cub, then went on to the "Yellow Peril" at San Antonio, Pensacola or Livermore. Following that introduction, most if you went on to fly first line combat aircraft such as the Fortress, Lightning or the Hellcat.

A few CPTP graduates continued to fly the Piper Cub in its military olive drab livery as the utility jack-of-all-trades L-4, spotting for an artillery battery, evacuating the wounded, firing rockets from strapped on bazookas or ferrying General "Blood and Guts" Patton around his command. You few earned your flight pay just as much as those flying the higher horsepower hot rods in combat.

All of you tell your fond memories of the venerable Piper Cub, a demanding but rewarding training aircraft, and after you returned from the wars and spent a few years you may have looked into acquiring your own Piper Cub. Many of you persisted and put a little yellow memory in your own hangar on a small grass field somewhere. I'm very happy for you.

I missed out on the Piper Cub, but spent thousands of hours in its big brother the Super Cub towing training gliders up to 3000 feet agl, shaking them off and falling out of the sky in a series of split Ss to give a another training tow. For two weeks of every year we towed high-performance gliders into the standing wave behind Mount Mitchell, and watched as they reached altitudes in excess of 30,000 feet.

The writer of this book, Jim Foreman, has been flying most of his life, starting with an accidental takeoff in another man's home built aircraft at age 14. His concerned father grounded young Jim until a few months before his 16th birthday, when he financed formal flying lessons that led to Jim's solo in a Piper Cub on that significant birth date.

In order to get enough flight time for a commercial license, young Jim paid his own way to the Piper Aircraft plant in Lock Haven, Pennsylvania to pick up and deliver Piper Cubs to their buyers around the United States. He credits those flights, without a radio or IFR panel, for a lot of his hard earned experience. After a tour with the Army in Korea, Jim spent some time ferrying surplus aircraft across the United States. Whether it was Vultee Vibrators or Lockheed Lightnings, Jim's motto was, "Show me how to start it, and I'll fly it." Ah, youth.

Jim retired to the Black Forest Glider port in Colorado, towing and flying sailplanes into the standing wave behind Pike's Peak, getting his Diamond Altitude Badge and helping many other "glider guiders" do the same. He did his tows with the Super Cub, we have that in common.

I thoroughly enjoyed the three stories that follow and I'm sure that you will also.

Kent Hugus

FLIGHT THROUGH HISTORY

The clock on the bedside table read a quarter to midnight when the phone jangled me out of a deep REM sleep and the voice on the other end said, "Jim, I just bought a restored J-3 Cub from a guy in Durango and could you bring it to me?"

I'm not sure what I mumbled in my stupor but he continued, "Sorry for calling you this late, this is John in Oshkosh. I'll call you in the morning with details."

I fell back into the arms of Morpheus wondering two things, how was I going to get to Durango and how was I going to get a plane with less than a 10,000 foot service ceiling over those 12,000 mountain passes.

I was far more coherent when John's call came the next morning and answered both questions; the guy had agreed to deliver it to Black Forest. "It's been rebuilt from the ground up and is just like a brand new airplane," he explained, adding that it would be there the next day. What he didn't mention was that it hadn't been flown since being rebuilt.

There it sat in the middle hangar at the gliderport, brilliant Cub yellow with a black electric stripe running from the engine with cylinders poking out in the air to the bear emblem askew on the fin. Looked just like it did the day it rolled out of the green building at Lock Haven. I noticed the registration numbers, N-99998. They seemed strangely familiar but I passed it off as just being an awfully good poker hand.

Two men were just finishing the task of installing the wings. He had solved the problem of getting it to me by hauling it over the mountains on a trailer. I met the owner who told me that he had been a crew chief on a B-17 during WW-II and had been wanting to learn to fly ever since. However, he had just been diagnosed with cancer and wouldn't be around long enough to do much of anything. He was selling the airplane as part of clearing up his affairs before he passed on.

He had found this airplane as a basket case and spent the last seven years painstakingly restoring it back to new condition. Then he dropped the bomb; he wasn't an aircraft mechanic and the ship hadn't been flown. He did temper my shock a bit by telling me that his neighbor, who was a licensed mechanic, had helped him quite a bit and had signed off all the repairs in the logbooks. I spent the rest of the day going over the ship with a fine-tooth comb, checking every bolt, nut, cotter key and safety wire. I felt a lot better when I didn't find a single thing amiss.

He told me that the engine had the required two hours of ground running time since being remanufactured by a certified engine shop. After operations had ceased at the gliderport, I took it up for a test flight. I hadn't flown a Cub in perhaps thirty years but I did have skads of time in its big brother, the Super Cub.

It flew surprisingly well with the left wing just slightly down in level flight. A turn on the left strut turnbuckle solved that. I'd flown a number of new airplanes out of the factory so what was the difference, I reasoned. I filled the 12-gallon fuel tank to the brim, rolled it into the hangar and closed the door. I wanted to be off at daybreak the next morning.

Even though I had aviation charts, I decided to turn this into a nostalgic adventure by using Texaco road maps for navigation like we did when the ship was built in 1946. After all, it had no radio so most of the information on the charts would be useless anyway. I'd be navigating by roads and highway maps show them better than aviation charts.

The 65 horsepower engine would carry me along at a solid 60 miles per hour while burning about four gallons of fuel an hour, so with only a 12-gallon tank, 180 miles would be the absolute range. For comfort, it was better that they be no more than 150 miles apart. The first known airport in a direct line was McCook, Nebraska, 250 miles away but with no airports across northeastern Colorado, I would have to go straight east to Burlington and then back toward my course. I called a friend in Omaha, Nebraska and told him I'd spend the night there and would he meet me at a small airport where they flew gliders.

It was three days before Thanksgiving and several degrees below freezing when I rolled the ship out the next morning. I strapped my backpack under the belt in the front seat and tossed a set of tiedown ropes and a couple quarts of oil in the small luggage bin behind the back seat. I had some snacks and a bottle of water in the pockets on either side of my backpack so they would be easy to reach in flight. I had my doubts whether the engine would start on a cold morning so I pumped the primer three or four shots, pulled the prop through a couple times and turned on the switch. One pull and the little engine puttered happily to life. That was reassuring.

After the engine warmed enough to run smoothly at power, I checked the mags and went rolling down the runway. The little engine that produced 65 horsepower at sea level would only crank out about 45 at the 7,200 feet elevation where we were. After a long takeoff roll to build up flying speed, I lifted into the air, did a cropduster turn at fifty feet above the ground and headed east just as the sun poked its head above the horizon. No need to climb any higher because the ground dropped away to the east and every mile put me higher above the ground.

I glanced at the compass in the middle of the Spartan instrument panel and it read east. I hadn't checked it before I left so turned to the south; it still read east. A one-eighty back to the north and the compass still read east. Then I noticed the heads of the four screws holding it in the panel; they were silver; steel instead of brass. The magnet in the compass was locked onto the steel screws and wasn't about to move. No problem, there were section lines and roads to follow.

In addition to the non-working compass, there were the two engine gauges on the right, one with dual hands showing oil pressure and temperature and the other the tachometer. Oil pressure was 20 psi and the temp was barely above the peg. Even in midsummer temps the oil never got much above 200 degrees but on a cold morning like this, it would never get above just warm. The engine was running smoothly at 2150 rpm.

On the far left was the airspeed indicator and next to it the altimeter, neither of which were really useful in a ship like that. It would only go 60 miles an hour and you could guess at how high you were. In fact, since you flew the Cub from the back seat, a student never saw any of the instruments until the instructor climbed out and he went solo.

The only other gauge was a piece of wire sticking out of the gas cap in front of the windshield. There was a joke that it didn't tell you how much fuel you had, but how much you didn't have. It was just a big cork on the bottom of a piece of wire. It stuck up about six inches when the tank was anything more than half full and only moved down when you were less than that. When the bend in the wire hits bottom, you were supposed to have fifteen minutes of fuel remaining. What it really meant was when it started moving down, you needed to start looking for an airport. When it hit bottom, you'd better have found one.

The Cub was the ultimate in simplicity. The ignition switch is above the left window where it could be reached from either seat as well as seen by the person cranking the ship so he could assure himself whether it was on or off before he touches the prop. There was a throttle lever for each seat and just above the left toe of the rear pilot was a pair of knobs, one which turned heated air to the carburetor in case of ice forming and a the other the cabin heat. There was also a crank that looked like it was made to raise and lower the windows in an old Ford that operated the trim tab so the ship would fly level. The Cub was rather trim sensitive and had to be adjusted about every fifteen minutes as each gallon of fuel was burned out of the tank.

Small eastern Colorado towns with strange names crept beneath the wings as I motored into the rising sun. It was warm on my face but the cold air whistling in around the window and door made the down jacket I was wearing feel very comfortable. My feet were cold even though the cabin heater was on. About all it would warm is the right foot of someone in the front seat.

I flew over a woman who was feeding chickens in the yard by scattering grain she carried in a pan. She looked up and waved. I rocked my wings. A bit further along I spotted a pickup truck chasing a cow across the prairie. The cow kicked up puffs of yellow dust each time its feet hit the ground and a cloud of dust boiled from under the pickup as it bounded across the rough ground. The cow surged down into a gully and up the other side as the pickup skidded to a stop. The cow stopped and turned around as if to say in cow language, "Can't catch me!"

Nearly an hour had passed and Limon began to grow in the windshield. A little closer and I could see the golden arches of McDonalds at the exit from the interstate. I had left without breakfast, so a cup of coffee and an Egg McAnything would taste great right now. The Limon airport was a couple miles away but no one was ever there. I even considered landing in a wheat field nearby, but settled for some water and cheese crackers from my backpack.

Seventy-five miles and eight small towns lay between Limon and Burlington, nothing to do but watch the cars as they passed me on the four lane below. Occasionally one would spot me flying at about 500 feet and flash their headlamps. Wheat fields are all a mile square so I clicked my watch as I passed over one fenceline and stopped it at the next. Fifty-nine seconds; sixty-one miles an hour, not even a breath of a tailwind to help me along. At least there was no headwind either. Each town had a tall, white grain elevator and I could always count at least three towns ahead.

Two and a half hours in the air, I turned a short final and glided over the interstate to land at the Burlington Airport. Chirp, chirp, bounce, bounce, bounce. I had forgotten how difficult it is to make a smooth landing in a Cub with its fat tires that want to bounce like basketballs. As I rolled to a stop at the fuel pump and killed the engine, a pickup truck came roaring up. "I was having breakfast at the DQ when I saw you landing. Nice looking Cub you have there," he said as he handed me a cup of DQ coffee and dragged the hose over to the ship. I finished the coffee, hit the bathroom, thanked him and paid for ten gallons of fuel. It was burning four gallons an hour, right on the dot. He spun the prop and I was back in the air after no more than fifteen minutes on the ground.

A hundred twenty miles, two hours, and no roads or railroad to follow from Burlington to McCook, Nebraska. Just head off at about a 45-degree angle to the section lines and you can't miss it. Two highways cross at McCook so if you hit either of them, just follow it to town. Besides, you can see the two big white grain elevators twenty miles before you get there.

While a boy less than half the age of the Cub pumped eight gallons into the tank, he looked inside and asked, "Where's the radio?"

"Doesn't have one." "How do you know where you're going," he asked.

"Just follow the map," I replied as I headed for the office.

"Anything to eat here?" The guy behind the counter motioned toward a freezer. Inside were frozen hamburgers, hot dogs and burritos. I nuked a hamburger in the microwave and took a bag of chips from a box. No breakfast and now this for lunch. I filled my water bottle and was back in the air because it was over four hours and another fuel stop at Grand Island before Omaha.

I checked the weather while fueling at Grand Island. A cold front had stalled out across the area and Lincoln was reporting low clouds with light snow while fifty miles to the north, Columbus and Omaha were clear. A bit of a detour but not much so I followed Highway 30 to the northeast. It wasn't long before scuddy clouds to the right pushed me further north.

I'd been in the air a bit over an hour when I finally made it around the end of the low clouds and turned east toward Columbus. The sun was sinking rapidly toward the western horizon and I began to doubt that I would be able to make it Omaha before sunset. I'd still have enough light to land up to half an hour after sunset.

I heard a few quick chirps from the engine and suddenly it began to shake and the rpm dropped to about 1700. I could tell that it was running on only three cylinders and knew that there was not enough power to keep me in the air. A small town lay just ahead and I had enough altitude to reach it. I wanted to land as near help as possible and figured I could find a suitable field near there. I looked along the roads leading out of town because I knew if they had an airstrip of any sort, it would be next to one of them. Sure enough, about a mile from town I spotted a grass strip with a hangar next to it.

I tied the ship down and found the problem immediately. The top sparkplug on the left rear cylinder had unscrewed and was hanging on the plug wire behind the cylinder. The good thing was that it hadn't fallen off but the bad thing was that particular plug was the hardest one to get to. In order to tighten that plug, the cowling and the baffles that direct air over the cylinders would have to be removed.

I knocked at the door of a house across the road from the airport and asked the lady if she knew who ran the airport. She invited me inside and called someone. A few minutes later a pickup pulled up outside. It turned out that he had an airplane in the hangar and was a tractor dealer in Genoa where I had landed. I told him the problem with the engine and that I needed a room for the night and something to eat. I also needed to call my friend in Omaha so he didn't scramble the CAP to search for me when I didn't arrive. I got my backpack out of the ship and just before closing the door, I also took the fat envelope containing the ship's papers out of the luggage bin. For some reason, people rummaging through an airplane will take the logbooks and other papers even though they are totally useless to them but absolutely essential to have with the airplane.

Genoa has a motel of sorts. A man had closed off his two-car garage, put a wall down the middle to make two rooms, which he rented. They shared a common bath. The people were leaving just as we arrived so they told me to make myself at home and leave ten dollars on the dresser. Then we went to the only cafe in town where I could also make my phone call. After I finished dinner, he handed me the keys to his pickup and said, "I just live a block away, meet me here in the morning for breakfast."

There was no TV or anything to read in the room so I opened up the packet of the ship's papers. Sure enough, there was a stack of FAA Form 337s covering all the repairs made during the rebuilding process as well as a number covering the years before. I started thumbing through the logbooks to trace the history of the ship. The last time it had been flown was fifteen years before when it had been damaged by a windstorm. It had been sitting for a long time and gone through three owners before the man who rebuilt it. Further back it had belonged to a flying school who trained people under the GI Bill. There were several notations of repairs after students had either ground looped it and damaged a wing or used the brakes too hard and stood it on its nose. I flipped to the first pages of the original logbook and was shocked to see the name of the pilot who had flown it from Lock Haven to Wes-Tex Aircraft in Lubbock, Texas; it was me! No wonder the registration numbers had seemed so familiar. The other interesting thing was that the flight began on the same day as today except 40 years before in 1946. I had flown perhaps half a dozen new planes out of the factory in those days while building the required 200 hours to get my commercial license. Things were a bit different then; a person paid their own way to the factory just to get the flying time.

It was just getting gray in the east when I arrived the next morning to find him already there, reading a newspaper and having coffee. As I sat down, he shoved a strange looking wrench across the table to me. It took me a few seconds to realize what it was. It was a special wrench made just for tightening the top plugs on Continental engines. "Where in the world did you get this?" I asked.

"A fellow who works for me used to work on airplanes years ago and when I explained your problem, he dug through a tool box and came up with it."

With the special wrench it took only a couple minutes to screw the plug back in and tighten it, something that would have taken an hour or longer without it. I checked the rest of the plugs while I was at it and found two others that were loose and might have come out at some point. It's amazing the strange things that one can forget when doing repairs.

I thanked my benefactor and four fuel stops later, the last some fifty miles out of Oshkosh during which I called John and told him to notify the tower that I would be arriving without a radio. The FAA rule is that the only way one is allowed to land at an airport with a control tower is to notify them by phone no more than an hour or less than half an hour before your arrival. They want to know the direction you will be coming from so they can watch for you.

The tower turns their rotating white and green beacon on

at sunset and I was at least ten miles out when I spotted it. At three or four miles away I saw the lights on their main runway go off and those for a shorter one across the north end come on, indicating the runway which they wanted me to use. Then they shot me a green light from the tower. I rocked my wings in acknowledgment, flew a short pattern and touched down on the runway. I saw a car coming toward me, flashing his lights. Then it turned around and led me to John's hangar. Sixteen and a half hours in the air, I was cold, hungry, tired and ready to get out of that airplane. Somehow flying a Cub seemed a lot more fun when I was eighteen than now that I was fifty-eight.

I flew back from Milwaukee early on Thanksgiving morning with the plans to hop in the Cessna 210 and fly on to Texas where my wife was already with her sister. The only problem was when we arrived at Colorado Springs, the snow was coming down and I knew it was much heavier in the forest which was 2000 feet higher elevation.

With the gliderport closed, there was no way I could call someone to come after me so I hopped a cab. The higher we climbed toward the trees, the worse the roads became until half a mile from the house, he could go no further and I had to trudge through the snow from there. I wrote this story as a magazine article which was ultimately published in Plane and Pilot, then with nothing else to do other than watch the snow come down, I decided to write a novel about the flight. During the next four days while the snow piled up to more than three feet deep, I let my mind run a little wild. The result was The Flight.

THE FLIGHT

CHAPTER ONE

The glowing numbers on the clock radio on the bedside table read 11:57PM as I hung up the phone but being half awake, half asleep and totally confused, I wasn't sure whether I had just talked with a friend in Wisconsin or if it was just a dream telling me that I needed to wake up and go to the bathroom. I thought about calling him back but decided that if he hadn't called, he would think that I must be drunk or crazy, or both, to wake him up in the middle of the night. Tomorrow morning would be soon enough and I would be in better condition to understand what he had said about needing a restored Piper J-3 Cub delivered.

At an age where most men are just hitting their peak, I suddenly found myself among the gainfully unemployed, otherwise known as retired, after having been given the golden handshake by a company which had extracted the best twenty years of my life. However, one of the good things about no longer being tied to a nine to five schedule, I was now able to pursue the fun things of life which I had been forced to place on hold for many years. One of the activities that I enjoyed, but one which would hardly produce the income necessary to support a family, was flying. I now had the opportunity to spend as much time in the air as I wished by flying towplanes at the local gliderport and ferrying airplanes around the world.

I made my first solo flight on my sixteenth birthday in 1944 in a Piper Cub, and having begun flying at that particular period of time, I was able to build up a considerable amount of experience in airplanes which today's pilots know only from photos or in museums.

Piper Aircraft began building the Cub in 1936, right in the middle of the worst of the depression years. With all the other aircraft companies building heavy biplanes powered by engines of 200 or more horsepower, the frail looking Cub appeared almost as a joke. It was powered by a Tinker Toy four cylinder engine advertised as producing forty horsepower. The little engine had two rather highly debatable points: horsepower and dependability. When it was running at top efficiency, the Cub would putter along at about fifty miles an hour. With the price for a brand new Cub at $699.00, it became the Tin Lizzie of the air and within the affordable range of a lot of people.

Gasoline was selling for nineteen cents a gallon in those days which meant that one could fly a Cub for an hour for about half a dollar. Even during the depression years, this put the cost of flying within the reach of many people. Two years later, a much more dependable sixty-five horsepower engine was fitted which boosted the speed of the Cub to sixty miles an hour and making it an instant favorite for training purposes. Piper produced a steady stream of bright yellow Cubs from their Lock Haven, Pennsylvania plant until the war began, at which time they changed the color to Army Drab and began shipping them overseas by the thousands where they were used by forward observes to direct artillery fire. They built the last of the venerable J-3 Cubs in 1948. With a slightly larger engine, it was produced as the PA-ll for a couple more years.

Piper reintroduced the basic design in 1956, calling it the Super Cub. The new version was considerably heavier and powered by a much larger engine. Other refinements made it able to fill the need for an airplane which could be used for spraying crops and towing gliders. At a time when every other airplane on the market had sprouted nose wheels for much easier ground handling, the Super Cub remained a "Taildragger" and was just as demanding to fly as had been its grandfather. Due to the level of attention needed to fly the Cub, there grew an old saying that if one could fly a Cub well, he could fly just about anything.

Most people who have learned to fly in the past 40 years have done so in airplanes with a nose wheel and controls much like a car. One of the main differences in these airplanes and those like the Cub is as soon as the wheels are on the ground, the flight is over and all that is left is to "drive" it to the ramp.

Getting the wheels on the ground on a ship with a tailwheel only begins the landing process, they must be controlled all the way, because having a center of gravity behind the main wheels, they are somewhat unstable and require constant attention to keep them rolling straight. Also, taxiing requires use of both rudder and brakes.

Many pilots who learned to fly in a nosewheel airplane have a great amount of difficulty in making the transition to one with a tailwheel. The other disconcerting aspect is that they are no longer sitting on the left like in a car and steering with their left hand but in a tandem arrangement and flying with their right hand on a stick.

When I called John the following morning, he apologized for having called at such a late hour and said that indeed, he had bought a restored 1946 J-3 Cub from a man in western Colorado and needed it delivered. The former owner would arrange to have it brought to Black Forest but he needed someone who he could trust to fly it on to Oshkosh. We agreed on a price for the delivery and the deal was set.

This was going to be a fun trip, flying along a few hundred feet above the ground with the door open, enjoying the fresh air in my face and waving at people on the ground. It would be just like the old days when I was a kid and people flew just for the fun of it. Flying had now become either a job or a way to get from one point to the other and most of the pure enjoyment of flying had been lost. These days, when a pilot lands he simply rolls the ship into the hangar, closes the door and goes home. No longer do they stand around the hangar and talk about the experience. Hangar flying is a lost art.

CHAPTER TWO

There it sat, bright yellow in the morning sunlight, looking as if it had just rolled out the door of the big green factory building on the banks of the Susguehanna River. A black electric stripe ran from just beneath the exposed cylinders of the 65 horsepower Continental engine, back to the tail where a slightly askew decal of a bear held the Cub emblem. Piper put their decals on in a strange way, they weren't straight either with the ship sitting on the ground or in level flight

I ran my hand over the varnished wooden propeller and marveled at the excellent job that had been done in restoring the ship to its original condition. He had paid great attention to the most minute details. I was amazed to find that the ship was still fitted with the original fat, slick, bouncy tires and a tiny hard rubber tailwheel. I hadn't seen either of those on an airplane in years.

Rather than having twelve inch high registration numbers on the sides of the fuselage as is the accepted practice today, the numbers were in the same location as when the ship was built. It had huge 24" numbers on top of one wing and bottom of the other with small numbers on either side of the tail. The ship had a rather unique registration number, N99998. One more and it would have been all nines. For some reason, I kept getting the strange feeling that I had seen that particular number before, but I finally passed it off as simply being a killer poker hand.

The door on the Cub doesn't swing open like most other airplanes. It is split along the middle with the window half raising up to a hook on the lower surface of the right wing while the lower half simply drops down against the side of the fuselage. It has no outside handle and to open or close it from the outside, one has to slide open the window on the left and reach across the front seat to turn the handle from the inside. One of the benefits of a door of this design is that the window can be left open in flight for some ventilation or both it and the door for a lot. Opening the lower half gives the pilot in the back seat much better visibility when landing and was probably the first stall warning indicator to be found on an airplane. Just before the wing stalls, the increased angle of attack of the air flowing along the side of the fuselage will lift the door. Old time instructors knew of this and would always close the lower door to keep students from depending on it to tell them when the ship was about to stall.

The instrument panel was totally original, containing only the basic gauges required when the ship was built. To the far left side of the panel was the tachometer and to the far right was the combination oil pressure and temperature gauge. Both of these instruments bore the original Cub markings. The reason for separating the engine instruments to either side of the panel was so the pilot in the rear seat could see them around a person in the front seat. The compass, airspeed and altimeter were clustered together in the middle of the panel and totally hidden by a passenger or the instructor in the front seat. I can remember that it was on my first solo flight that I was able to see how high I was or how fast I was going. Pilots in those days were taught to control their speed by a combination of wind noise, stick pressure and nose attitude. The altitude was estimated by how large things looked on the ground.

The ignition switch was located above the left window so it could be reached from either seat and to make it visible to whoever was cranking the engine. It's a great comfort to a person pulling the propeller to be able to see the position of the switch rather than having to depend on what the pilot might tell him. Everything else in the cockpit was just as it had been in 1946 except that a fuel selector valve had been added just below the knob for the carburetor heat. Normally, the Cub carried only 12 gallons of fuel in a tank just in front of the instrument panel. With the original 40 horse engine burning less than three gallons an hour, they ship had well over four hours range. They didn't increase the tank size when they installed the larger engine and with it burning about four gallons an hour, you were going to be on the ground every three hours, one way or another. With a cruising speed of only 60 miles per hour, fuel stops could be no more than about 180 miles apart.

The fuel gauge on the main tank was simply a piece of cork attached to a wire which protruded through a hole in the filler cap. As the fuel level went down, so did the wire. The length of the wire was adjusted so that when it hit bottom, there was about 15 minutes of fuel left in the tank. During the Cub's 40 years of life, someone had installed an additional tank in the left wing, doubling the amount of fuel which could be carried. I still wouldn't consider 300 miles as being a long range for an airplane, but for something so slow it couldn't keep up with trucks on the highway, it would be just great duration. There are very few pilots who are old enough to have flown Piper Cubs and still have bladders which can last for five hours.

I finished the preflight, removed the tiedown ropes from the wings and propped the engine. It came to life on the first pull and ticked over smoothly. The Cub has no parking brake so I put a pebble in front of each tire to prevent it from rolling away when I untied the rope holding the tail.

Getting into either seat in a J-3 requires a certain amount of gymnastics and no two people seem to do it the same way. If one doesn't go about getting into the Cub correctly, he will usually find himself with one or both feet hanging out the door and no way short of breaking bones to get them inside.

I was thankful that the Cub is flown solo from the back seat because the front seat is extremely uncomfortable for anyone much over about five feet tall. One of the things that Piper did when they built the Super Cub was to move both seats back several inches to give the pilot in the front seat more leg room and comfort. Not only is there considerably more padding in the rear seat, the back extends higher and wraps around the shoulder blades.

The long control stick appears totally out of proportion with the rest of the ship. It s well over an inch in diameter and stands almost as high as the backrest of the front seat. It's fitted with a big, rubber grip like something normally found on the handles of a wheel barrow. I wouldn't be surprised if that's not where it came from. The stick is so long that the pilot's knuckles are against the backrest of the front seat when it is fully forward and tucked into his stomach when all the way back for landing. A pilot with much of a belly has quite a problem getting the stick all the way back. With the lack of any aerodynamic balancing of the control surfaces, that extra leverage of the long stick does come in handy at times.

I nudged the throttle forward and the engine responded smoothly. The fat tires rolled over the pebbles and we waddled off toward the runway like a big yellow duck. I left the door open so I could enjoy the beautiful morning. After a quick check of the magnetos, I pulled the carburetor heat on and the engine RPM dropped. Satisfied that the little ship was ready to fly, I pointed the nose down the runway and shoved the throttle forward to the stop. There was no surge of power and noise like the big 180 HP engines on the towplanes, just a comfortable increase in speed and soon the tail came up to where I could see over the nose. Before lifting the ship off the runway, I made my usual engine instrument check, both oil gauges in the green and 2100 RPM. The Cub is the ultimate in simplicity.

There was a solid feel to the stick in my hand. It took both pressure and movement to get results, not like the present crop of airplanes which are more like driving a car with power steering than flying an airplane. I had forgotten just how honest the Cub flies. It is totally predictable in that it does exactly the same thing every time. In steep turns, the nose tracks around the horizon with no tendency to rise or dive. No matter what attitude the ship is in when it is stalled, the warning and break are always the same. It spun with enthusiasm but would recover instantly when told to do so. The Cub is simply one of those rare airplanes which has no unusual quirks or surprises.

It was like shaking hands with an old friend as we danced with the puffy white clouds for the better part of an hour. I had almost forgotten what true flying is all about. I entered the landing pattern on downwind, pulled carburetor heat and closed the throttle. The engine was ticking over so quietly that I gave it a little shot of power on crosswind just to be sure that it was still alive. It responded instantly. I turned final and picked a landing spot near the hangars, no use landing at one end of the runway and having to taxi all the way to the other. My landing spot began to sink slowly as viewed over the nose, indicating that I would overshoot slightly. I lowered the right wing and applied a bit of left rudder, pushing the Cub into a slip to the right. The wind rushed into my face through the open door and the glide angle became steeper.

The nose rose slowly and the sound of air over the wings diminished as we slowed and sank to within inches of the ground. The open door began to rise, telling me that I was approaching a stall. With the stick tucked firmly into my stomach, I felt the tailwheel touch first then the fat tires kissed the runway with quick little chirps. No skip, no bounce, no hippity-hop; they just began to roll. Best landing I ever made in a Cub!

I checked the oil, filled both tanks with fuel then tied the ship down. It was ready to take me anywhere I cared to point it. The only real problem with flying this ship any distance is that it is so terribly slow. The factory claims that it will cruise 80 miles per hour, but there is no way that it will go a bit above 65, even with the throttle wide open.

I called Flight Service to check the weather between Colorado and Wisconsin and found that a slow-moving weather system was hanging around over the plains and it would be two or three days before it would move out and leave a window of good weather. It makes a lot more sense to wait at home while the system moves than to fly up against it and have to wait it out at some strange airport. I turned to have one final look at the beautiful little ship before I walked away and suddenly those four nines and an eight of the registration number came back to haunt me. There was just something about them that I couldn't get out of my mind. I began to wonder where that ship had been all of its life, so I removed the large envelope containing the log books and other papers from the baggage compartment behind the back seat and took it home with me.

CHAPTER THREE

The log books of an airplane are its recorded history because they were written at the time certain things happened instead of after the fact. While the intended purpose of a log book is to record the fact that required inspections and repairs had been accomplished in the proper manner, but like a ship's log, other bits and pieces of information often find their way onto the pages. The historical record of the Cub filled four books, so I decided to begin with the present and work backward in time. All the entries in the newest log book were by the man who had bought the ship as a basket case some seven years before for five hundred dollars then spent thousands of hours lovingly rebuilding it.

In chronological order after buying the ship, it told how each piece was carefully restored to original condition. It told when and where each part was obtained and how much it cost. Every single bolt, nut and screw was replaced during the rebuilding. It even told how many coats of paint where sprayed on to give it a finish superior to what it had when new. The owner wasn't a licensed airplane mechanic, however he had one inspect and sign off each step of his work. From the log book entries, one could tell that he was an artist, with both wrenches and words. He had also restored the engine to like-new condition before it was mounted on the ship. The last entry in the log book simply said, "Could not pass FAA Medical due to heart condition, will have to sell ship." The mechanic who supervised the rebuilding of the ship did the test flight when it was completed and then delivered it to me.

Working backward through the log books, I found that before the Cub was sold to the man who did the restoration, it had languished for some six years in a barn in Kansas after a farmer bought it with the thought of returning it to airworthy condition but just never got around to it. Prior to being hauled to Kansas by the farmer, it had served as an advertising sign at a used car lot in Phoenix. The last record of the Cub having been flown was about fifteen years before when it was owned by a man who used it to spot fish for commercial fishermen in Oregon. It was during that period of time that the additional fuel tank was installed in the left wing to extend its duration. At one time, floats had been installed and it was flown as a seaplane in the Seattle area.

Reading the history of the ship was like reading a good novel, something that one once started, was difficult to put down. When I finally reached the original log book which came with the ship when Piper sold it, I noticed that it began its long life in a GI Flight Training School in Lubbock, Texas. There were several entries pertaining to repairing wingtips after students had ground looped it, propellers replaced after having been put up on the nose by unwise application of the brakes and a complete recover after being pounded by a West Texas hail storm.

I flipped to the front of the book and the first entry was dated August 10, 1946 by the production test pilot who flew it for twenty minutes and made a notation that the tires needed air. The next entry was for 29 hours for the ferry flight from Lock Haven to Lubbock, Texas. I couldn't believe my eyes, but the signature on that entry was mine! I had made the original delivery flight of the ship. In fact, in three days it would be the 40th anniversary of the date that I departed the factory in Lock Haven, bound for Lubbock.

I was seventeen years old at the time and was doing everything that I could in order to build up the required 200 hours of flying time so I could apply for my commercial pilot's license as soon as I became eligible on my eighteenth birthday. I remembered that I had been so desperate for flying time that I even offered to pay for my own transportation to the Piper factory if Wes Tex Aircraft would pay for the fuel and allow me deliver new ships to them.

I still remember that epic flight. The summer of 1946 was an especially rainy one with almost constant low clouds and thunderstorms along the route. I had to sit and wait for flyable weather so many times that it took me fifteen days to fly from Pennsylvania to Texas. That was also the year that I began my senior year in high school and missed the first four days due to the delays in getting home.

Here was my chance for a trip into nostalgia, a return to those salad days of my youth when my short attention span alternated between girls and airplanes. While I would not be flying the Cub back to its home in Lock Haven, at least I would be headed in the proper direction. Even though stiff knees would begin to protest being in the same position for too long a period of time and my lower back would remind me that my 60th birthday was only a couple years down the road, I would fly with the door to my youth open and let the air blow through my graying hair.

Back in 1946, flying charts sold for fifty cents each and enough of them to cover the area from Pennsylvania to Texas would set a person back four or five dollars. To a high school student in those days, that was a considerable amount of money but fortunately, there was an alternative which cost nothing. Texaco was the only company which refined aviation gasoline in those days and to advertise that fact, the location of every airport in the nation was shown on their road maps. Not only could a pilot locate an airport easily on a road map, the need to carry a ruler was eliminated because they also listed the mileage between towns. About the only pilots who actually bought flying maps were those who had enough money to afford to wear genuine Ray Ban sunglasses own a real pilot's chronograph with four buttons on it. In those days, I had neither. I had used Texaco road maps when I flew the Cub from Lock Haven to Lubbock, so I would use them on this trip.

The local Texaco distributor agreed to furnish me with road maps for Colorado, Kansas, Nebraska, Iowa and Wisconsin and to my surprise, they still indicated the location of airports at many of the smaller towns. It's a nice touch and helps fill up space, especially across Kansas where there isn't much else to show. After picking up the maps, I dropped by the bank to draw some money for the trip. I cashed a check for $500 which would cover both the expenses of getting the ship there as well as the cost of an airline ticket back. The bank teller counted out twenty-five crisp new twenty dollar bills and while I was there, I also picked up a ten dollar roll of quarters. Telephones, vending machines and just about every other coin operated machine requires or will accept quarters. Having a good supply of quarters in your pocket on a ferry flight is not only a good idea, but often a necessity.

A high pressure area was building over the plains states, forecasting fair weather and light winds. It would be ideal flying weather for several days. For ferry flights, I took along only the basic clothing which would be needed for the three or four days which I would be away from home. Everything could be stuffed inside a small backpack which was durable, easy to carry and did not need to be checked when I boarded an airliner. There is an old saying that there are only two kinds of luggage on an airliner, carry-on and lost.

I had intended to take along nothing which I would not have used in 1946 but since Oshkosh has a control tower and I might need to get into some other controlled airport, I decided to fudge a bit and take my portable, two-way aircraft radio. Flying into a controlled airport without a radio can be done but it requires landing at some other airport and calling the tower on the phone at least an hour ahead of your arrival to tell them what time and from which direction you will be approaching. If they happen to be in an agreeable mood that day, they will approve your request and give you a green light when you arrive.

Thanks to transistors and synthesized circuits, a battery-operated radio which is no larger than the average cordless telephone will cover all 720 aviation frequencies. While the six inch, "Rubber Ducky" antenna limits its range to about twenty miles, it is more than adequate to get into and out of airports. I slipped the radio into the backpack along with my clothing and shaving kit. Road maps don't list such information, so I jotted down the ATIS, approach and tower frequencies for Omaha, Des Moines and Oshkosh on the borders of the maps for those states.

Most pilots would say that my method of planning cross country flights is far too casual, but that's the way that I've done it for the past forty years. I simply lay a ruler from where I am to where I'm going to establish the basic direction. On this flight, it will be a compass heading of about 60 degrees. This also means that I will be crossing east-west lines at about a 30 degree angle to the left. Country roads and property lines run square with the world just about everywhere except down around Odessa, Texas where east is based on the point where the sun rises above the horizon on June 21st, the longest day of the year. It has something to do with Spanish land grants.

The distance from Black Forest to Oshkosh is a tad over 900 miles which at 60 miles an hour, is two very long flying days or three shorter ones. I'll plan for two long days and see how it works out as I go along. McCook, Nebraska is about half way to Omaha and will make a good place to stop for fuel and stretch my legs. If I can make it all the way to Omaha before dark, I'll be able to spend the night with friends. I called John to let him know that unless the weather changed, I would depart the following morning.

CHAPTER FOUR

I called the Flight Service in Denver to get an update on the weather along my intended route. The forecast called for severe clear all the way to Oshkosh for the next two days with the only possible exception being a very weak low pressure trough laying on a north-south line across Nebraska. They added that it was so weak that probably the only result would be an increase in southerly winds along it. Other than that, winds were forecast to be more or less calm along the route.

I had a quick breakfast and was at the airport just as the sun poked above the horizon. The luggage compartment behind the back seat of the Cub is nothing more than a canvas bag covered by a hinged plywood lid with a hole about the size of a quarter in the middle of it. The hole is to stick your finger in and lift the lid. The luggage compartment was too small to accommodate my luggage and with no passenger, I wanted to get as much weight forward as possible so I put the backpack in the front seat and secured it with the seatbelt. Since it would take a circus contortionist to get anything out of the luggage compartment in flight, I stuffed my water bottle, two piddle packs and an apple into the pocket on the backrest of the front seat.

Everything seemed to be in airworthy condition as I went through a preflight of the airplane. Even though I had topped the fuel tanks before tying the ship down, I removed the caps and stuck my finger into the opening to be sure that the fuel had not leaked out or that someone hadn't put in a hose and siphoned off some of it. It is not totally unknown to have someone hose off a tank of gas from an airplane which is tied down outside. Both tanks were still full so I opened the drain cock on the gascolator to dump any water that might have accumulated in the system. After pulling the engine slowly through each compression stroke to be sure that there were no leaking valves or rings, I pulled the engine through a few times with the throttle closed to pull some prime into the cylinders. With the magnetos on, I cracked the throttle slightly and gave the prop a pull. The little Continental responded instantly and fell into a sweet rhythm. It's always comforting when an engine starts on the first pull.

After letting the engine warm up, adjusting the altimeter to 7000 feet, the elevation of Black Forest Gliderport, and checking the magnetos, I rolled down the runway. With an airplane as simple as the Cub, there is very little to do prior to takeoff. At about 200 feet above the ground, I cranked the trim to level flight and swung the nose to the east. There was no reason to gain any more altitude because the ground drops off in that direction and the further that I flew, the higher I would be above the ground. Crossing the airport boundary, I made a 30 degree turn to the left to put Pikes Peak at my back and established a heading for my first stop at McCook.

I had taken off with the fuel selector on the nose tank but as soon as I was clear of the airport, I switched to the wing tank. That would keep all the weight possible forward for better trim and possibly an extra mile or so an hour of airspeed. Since the wing tank had no gauge, I would burn out of it first. The 10 gallons carried in the wing should provide at least three hours of fuel. My plan was to fly on the wing tank for two hours and then switch back to the nose tank. By doing it this way, should I have to run the nose tank dry, I would have something like an hour of reserve in the wing. It's not exact science on fuel management but better than a wild guess. I scanned the simple instruments; 2100 RPM, 7200 feet of altitude, 160 degrees oil temperature, 20 pounds oil pressure and 50 MPH indicated airspeed. With the airspeed corrected for the altitude, it would be about 60.

I had recently received one of those computer generated form letters which said that my name had been selected by a computer, along with two others, and one of us had won a new automobile. The two people who did not win the car would receive a valuable alternate prize. All I had to do in order to claim the automobile, or other valuable prize, was to visit their delightful RV resort and take a short tour of the facilities with one of their pleasant hosts. What this really meant was that I would have to submit myself to half an hour of a high pressure salesmanship trying to sell me a membership in an RV camping resort. I would learn if I was the lucky winner of the new car only after my tour at which time the salesman would remove the seal on my letter and expose the secret number.

After listening to the salesman's spiel while driving past empty RV parking spaces and seeing the pool and clubhouse under construction, I told him that I wasn't interested in buying a membership. He ripped the seal off my letter to disclose my secret number and guess what, I had missed winning the car by just one digit, but had won the valuable alternate prize, a combination wrist watch and electronic calculator just like ones that the NASA Astronauts wore. It must be true because there was a picture of the Space Shuttle and "NASA" on the plastic face of the watch. I would estimate that their cost for the watch was something less than three bucks. It just happened that the battery in my good watch had expired and I hadn't gotten around to having it replaced, so I strapped on my valuable prize.

It's truly amazing the number of functions which can be programmed into a simple silicon chip which couldn't cost more than a few cents. That cheap plastic watch would not only tell time, but by pressing certain buttons, would give you the time anywhere in the world. Alternating with the time function; it displayed the year, month, date and day of the week. It had a stop watch function, an elapsed time and alarm. It could remember 25 telephone numbers and the same number of birthdays anniversaries or other special events. It not only contained an eight digit calculator with all of the usual functions, but for pilots and astronauts, it could also compute time, distance and speed. Having nothing else to keep me occupied while I puttered along at a speed considerably less than that traveled by the astronauts in the space shuttle, I decided to test out the time, distance and speed function of the calculator.

According to the instructions, I pressed the tiny button marked "TDS" and "Distance" began to flash on the screen. I entered 1 mile and it began to blink "Time". As I passed over one section line fence, I pressed the "Start" button. When I crossed the next fence a mile away, I pressed the "Stop" button followed by the equals sign. Up came 59 seconds and a speed of 61 MPH. How about that, it actually works.

I checked the time in New York, London and Tokyo. It would have given me the square root of a number or multiply it by Pi had I asked. For the life of me, I couldn't come up with a single number for which I needed to know the square root, much less what it was when multiplied by Pi. No matter how little else one has to do, it's still awfully hard to maintain a high level of interest in a plastic watch with a picture of the Space Shuttle on it.

Flying three or four hundred feet above the ground at 60 miles an hour gives one a lot of time to observe things. I watched a man in a pickup truck chase a cow across the prairie. She crossed a deep ditch but he got stuck trying to follow her, so he got out and chased after her on foot. I don't know if he ever caught her. I saw a man riding a horse and he waved as I came closer. I rocked my wings in answer. Pilots used to rock their wings at people on the ground all the time but it had been years since I'd seen it done. I saw a woman hanging her wash on a clothes line to dry, but she didn't pay any attention to me. Either she didn't hear me or simply didn't care. There were sixteen white chickens and two red ones in her yard, they didn't seem to care either.

I checked my genuine NASA astronaut's watch and found that I had been in the air for two hours. I checked my ground speed, it was still 60 MPH. I had hoped for a tail wind to help me along but there was none. At least I could be thankful that there was no headwind. Even a little headwind really slows down a ship which is already going this slow. I'd swear that the seat cushion under me was a lot thinner and harder than it was when I took off. I shifted around, trying to find a more comfortable position, but it didn't help.

In late August, the whole world is brown. Wheat fields have long since been cut, leaving a brown stubble. The fields which have been turned under show brown earth and grass, which might have been green in the spring, has turned its own shade of brown. In Spanish, Colorado means a sort of rusty red color. Perhaps they should change the name of the state to Moreno, which means brown. The brown prairie rose over the horizon, marched slowly toward me and disappeared beneath my wings.

The sun had began to knock the chill from the morning air so I opened the door and latched the window against the bottom of the wing to allow the balmy August air flow in. I leaned my head out the door to sniff the hot air coming off the engine. It smelled of new paint. In the days of open cockpit airplanes, pilots learned how to tell the condition of their engines by how they smelled. The odor of carbon means that it is running too rich while a brassy smell means that it is too lean. Burning oil has its own odor and a rusty smell means that it is running too hot. The little Continental smelled just right.

Off to the north I can see the towns of Akron, Otis and Yuma. Behind me lay Deer Trail and Last Chance, and ahead was a place called Wray. The most prominent feature in each of these towns is the huge white grain elevator. I passed over a place called Beecher Island. How on earth could there be an island where there is no water? I puttered past by the towns of Cope, Joe, Kirk and Max; must have been settled by four brothers. I came to the conclusion that Eastern Colorado has more than its share of towns with funny names.

Total, sheer, abstract boredom is synonymous with flying cross country in a slow airplane. I could drive to Oshkosh in an automobile in about the same length of time that it will take me to fly there in the Cub. At least, on the ground, I would be able to read roadside signs advertising MacDonalds and the location of the world's deepest hand dug well at Oakley, Kansas. The Cub requires just enough attention to keep it level and on course to make reading a book out of the question. I've read a lot of books while the gyros, servos and gears of an automatic pilot tended to the flying chores. With a radar operator on the ground scanning the skies in front of me, there was little else to do. About the only thing to do in the Cub is give the trim handle half a turn about every half hour to keep it in trim as fuel is burned out of the nose tank.

I'd been in the air for better than three and a half hours when McCook, Nebraska finally came creeping over the horizon. I searched the landscape for the hangars which are always visible long before you can see the runways. Twenty minutes later I was entering downwind for a landing when the engine sputtered and began to windmill silently. I had forgotten to switch tanks after three hours. I moved the fuel selector to the nose tank and the engine came back to life. Looked as if my guess was right that four hours is the absolute maximum that I can get from the wing tank.

A young man, about the age that I was when I first soloed, walked from the office, "Put twenty dollars worth of 87 octane in the wing tank if it will hold that much."

"We don't have anything except 100 or Jet A," he replied.

"Then hundred octane will have to do, and please check the oil," I replied as I hobbled around on the ramp, trying to work the stiffness out of my knees before heading for the bathroom.

CHAPTER FIVE

I called Flight Service for a weather update and was told that every station to the east of McCook was reporting clear. I asked about the low pressure trough that the Denver Flight Service had mentioned as being across Nebraska. They told me that it was so weak that it had been dropped off the weather map two hours earlier, however a pilot had reported a few scattered low clouds west of Grand Island.

"Twenty dollars exactly filled the wing tank and the oil is OK," said the attendant as he walked in the door and handed me the fuel ticket.

"Anything to eat around here?" I asked.

"Crackers and candy are all, but you can use the courtesy car to go to a restaurant in town if you like," he replied.

I went over to the map on the wall and stretched the string to Omaha; it was 280 miles or just under five hours flying time. Having that extra tank would allow me to do it in one long hop. Navigation would be easy, angle a little more to the north until I picked up the interstate and follow it into Omaha. There was a small airport on the north side of the highway at the west edge of town. I had lost an hour on the clock when I crossed into the Central Time Zone, but if I got into the air immediately, I should still be able to make it to Omaha before sunset. I paid for the fuel and bought a candy bar.

"Could you give me a prop?" I asked the attendant.

"The boss says that our insurance won't allow me to hand crank an airplane, but if your battery is down, I'll bring the fuel truck over with some jumper cables."

"That wouldn't help any," I replied. "It doesn't have a starter either. Just stand against the elevator to keep the ship from rolling and I'll prop it."

As soon as I was off the ground, I established a cruising altitude of about 500 feet above the ground and took a heading which would intersect the interstate highway somewhere around Kearney, then I switched back to the wing tank. I was no more than twenty minutes east of McCook when I began to spot a few scattered clouds ahead. They seemed to be rather close to the ground, almost like ground fog. Evidently, the low pressure trough should have been left on the weather map. Things like that usually aren't very far across so I began to climb to see if I could see the other side of the clouds. At three thousand feet above the ground, I could see nothing except a solid deck of clouds all the way to the horizon. Beneath me, the spaces between the clouds were rapidly closing together. My first thought was to simply stay above the clouds and set a compass course for Omaha. I was bound to pass over them within an hour or so.

I hadn't even bothered to check the compass to see how it corresponded with known directions on the ground and decided that I should do so while I could still use section lines for reference. I headed east and the compass read East. I turned to the south but the compass remained on East. I finished the circle, leveling out to the west and then to the north, but the obstinate instrument refused to swing either way. It was immediately obvious why the compass would not respond; the heads of the attaching screws were silver in color, not brass. The magnets in the compass were locked onto those steel screws. Evidently the man who rebuilt the ship didn't know the difference and the mechanic who inspected it failed to notice them.

Even without a compass, I could have maintained an easterly course by keeping the sun to my right, but should something happen to the engine and I was forced to let down through the clouds, attempting to do so with no directional reference could turn into a fatal mistake. If a pilot enters clouds with no way of knowing whether he is turning or not, his life expectancy is whatever amount of time it takes for him to reach the ground at a very high rate of speed.

Had I flown the airplane long enough to come to trust the engine, I might have gone ahead, but with an unknown ship which had just recently been rebuilt, I was not ready to take that chance. The only other alternative, other than landing someplace and waiting for the clouds to burn off, was to see if I could get under them.

By checking the movement of the clouds against the ground, I estimated that the they were moving northward at about ten miles an hour, so that would be the logical direction to go in order to find the best conditions. I turned north and began to descend toward a fairly good size hole in the clouds. Circling down through the hole, I found that conditions beneath the clouds weren't too bad, about four hundred feet of ceiling and a good two miles visibility. It was damp and chilly beneath the clouds, making flight much more comfortable with the door closed. I established my 30 degree angle to the section lines and resumed my course for Omaha. Scud-running isn't my favorite sport in an airplane but at least I was making progress toward my destination.

I hadn't corrected for the wind drift to my left and reached the interstate sooner than I expected. I turned to follow it, staying directly above the right hand lanes, hoping that in case some other fool was coming from the opposite direction, he would be over the opposite lanes. There is one point of safety in flying directly above a road, you aren't likely to run into a radio tower.

Cars and trucks caught up with me and passed. Flying a Cub is one instance where it would be faster to drive than to fly. I hadn't progressed more than five or six miles before the clouds began to pinch closer to the ground and the visibility slowly reduced to less than a mile. It was getting too dicey to continue following the interstate and since conditions looked better to the left than they did straight ahead, I veered off in that direction.

Flying two or three hundred feet above the ground and being able to see only a couple miles make navigation very difficult. I was no longer trying to keep track of where I was, but simply flew in the direction where the clouds looked the lightest. I could fly four or five miles to the north and then be able to turn and go three or four to the east. At least I was making a certain amount of progress and if the band of clouds wasn't too wide, I should reach the other side before too long.

At one point, I flew over a farm airstrip and decided to land there, if for nothing more than to find out where I was and call for an update on the weather. I circled the house and burped the engine a few times, but no one came out. Even though no one appeared to be home, I began a short pattern to land when I flew through a flash of sunlight streaking down through a hole in the clouds. I thought that I must be getting near the eastern edge of the overcast, so I pulled up and headed out again. There is no use in landing if I will be in the clear before long.

I hadn't thought to check my watch when I took off or when I went under the clouds, so could only guess how long I had been in the air. It seemed like hours but I estimated it to be something over one hour but less than two. I pulled out the Nebraska map and tried to estimate where 75 to 90 miles in the general direction which I had been flying would put me. But since I had been flying either straight north or straight east most of the time, there was no way of knowing.

Droplets of water began to form on the windshield and a few seconds later, the engine began to lose power. Carburetor ice! I grabbed for the carburetor heat knob in an attempt to clear the ice from the intake manifold before it completely choked the engine. The outside air temperature does not need to be anywhere near freezing for carburetor ice to form once droplets of water begin to enter the system. Ice is caused by the cooling effect of the evaporating fuel in the carburetor and ice is most likely to form when the air temperature is around 68 degrees. All airplanes are subject to formation of carburetor ice, but the Cub seems to be one of the worst. It is probably because the heated air off the cylinders is routed outside of the cowling instead of around the carburetor.

Heated air to clear the ice is routed into the intake from a muff on the exhaust manifold, but the instant that the engine begins to lose power, the temperature of the exhaust drops and it becomes a race to melt the ice before the engine dies. The engine began to sputter and the RPM sagged to less than 1400, not enough power to keep me in the air. I looked for a place to land because from 200 feet of altitude, one has about 15 seconds before he is on the ground if total power is lost. I suddenly remembered the old trick of pumping the throttle to help break up the ice and tried that. The engine shuddered as if trying to help rid itself of the ice and slowly came back up to 1800 RPM, the maximum that it would turn because of the added restriction of the heat being on. I now had two problems, no forward visibility due to the water on the windshield and a loss of a good ten miles an hour speed.

I came to a paved road running east and west. It didn't appear to be a major highway of any sort, more like a Farm to Market road. Paved roads usually begin and end at a town of some sort so I turned to follow it. While I could see forward at an angle to either side, I had to swing the nose one way or the other to see where I was going. As I followed the road, I came to a pickup loaded with hogs parked on the edge of the pavement with a flat tire. The left front wheel was jacked up and the driver was trying to get the spare tire out of the wheel well in the front fender. The pickup must have dated to the mid-1930s because they never built one with the spare mounted in a front fender after the war. His head jerked up as I passed by a hundred feet high and I could see the surprise in his eyes. When I glanced back to see the grill on the pickup, I realized that it was a Hudson. The only place that sort of vehicle is seen is in antique automobile auctions. One in running shape, as this one obviously was, would bring up to ten thousand dollars. I wondered to myself why a person with such a rare and valuable antique would be using it to haul hogs.

I flew on for three or four miles and a small town began to materialize out of the drizzle. The highway which I was following became the main street of the town but returned to a farm road again at the other side. I guessed that the whole main street was no more than six or eight blocks from one end to the other. A squat, brick school building was on the south side of main street at the west edge of town. Four yellow school busses were parked behind the school, next to the bleachers for the football field. Along the four or five blocks between the school and the main intersection were mostly single story buildings until you came to the downtown intersection where two story brick buildings stood on all four corners. Another paved road ran north and south from the main intersection of town.

I spotted the courthouse which set a block off main street. It's always easy to pick out the courthouse in any small town as it is usually not only the largest, but also the ugliest building around. It seems that county commissioners are far more willing to spend tax monies for ugly buildings than they are when it comes to designing their own business buildings. I've never seen a bank, automobile dealership or any other private building which would match the average courthouse for lack of architectural grace. A water tower stood behind the court house and I could see that it had a name painted on it. I swung away from the main street so I could fly by the tower and read the name of the town.

The first thing that I saw as I approached the water tower was scrawled in big black letters, SRS-46. I can remember that the big thing each year when I was in high school was what they called the Junior-Senior flag fight. The two classes had an annual contest to see who could paint their flags in the most places as well as in the most visible or unusual places. The year that I was a senior, I borrowed an airplane which was equipped for sky writing and wrote SRS in the sky over the homecoming football game. They must not paint their water tower very often, I thought to myself.

SANGER, the name of the town, came into view as I circled past the tower. A sign on the red brick building across the street from the bank announced that it was a hotel and the decision was made, Sanger would be where I would wait for better weather.

There is an old saying that pilots killed in bad weather are usually buried in bright sunshine. I had pressed my luck far enough on this day.

I didn't bother to get the road map out to figure out where I was as there would be plenty time to do that later. The problem facing me now was to locate a safe place to land and secure the Cub. An airport would be the best choice but the Cub would be at home on most any level piece of ground. Lacking an airport, I would simply find a level field close to town where I could land, just like the barnstormers used to do.

From the air, I estimated the population of Sanger to be about a thousand people, give or take a few dogs. I wondered if it was large enough to have an airport. If they did have one, it would probably be located within a couple miles of town and most likely along one of the paved roads running out of town. I hadn't seen one on the way in from the west so that eliminated that direction.

I flew on past town to the east to check that direction and about a mile away, I saw three metal buildings which appeared to be airplane hangars on the right side of the road. As I came closer, I could also see a small office building, two parked airplanes and an orange windsock on a pole. I swung out, made a quick right turn and touched the wheels of the Cub down on the wet grass of the runway.

There were no cars at the airport and no one appeared when I killed the engine. I climbed from the Cub and walked through the slow drizzle to the tiny office building. The door was locked but a piece of paper taped to the window stated that one should call the Texaco station for fuel or call Harley Sloan for flight instruction or rides. Since I had no need for either of those services, I looked around for a place to tie the ship down. Three old airplane tires placed in a triangle in front of the office suggested the location of a tiedown spot but all that was there was short pieces of chain sticking out of the ground. There were no ropes and that was one of the things which I had forgotten to bring along.

The chilly drizzle was hitting me in the face as I walked to the two airplanes which were tied down on the south side of the hangars to see if there was anything there. I hadn't really paid any attention to the two ships when I landed and was rather surprised to find that one was a Waco Cabin biplane and the other was one of the nicest Fairchild PT-19s that I'd seen since the time when they were sold as surplus just after World War Two. A canvas cover was snapped in place over the open cockpits to keep the rain out. One of the greatest enemies to that particular ship was leaving the cockpits uncovered and allowing water to collect in the center section of the wing where it would begin to rot the wood and weaken the glue joints. The cockpit cover was usually one of the first things to be tossed aside by people when they bought the PT-19s as surplus from the War Assets Administration and they rapidly went from airworthy ships to airport eyesores. Deterioration of the wood in the center section of the wings is the reason why there are so few of that particular ship still around on the antique airplane market. The grass under both ships had been freshly mowed, indicating that they had been flown recently. There were no tiedowns other than the ones for those ships.

A little rain wouldn't harm the Cub but I certainly wasn't about to go off and leave it unsecured. While the wind was very light at the time, one never knew when it might increase. It takes only about 20 mph of wind to place a Cub in danger of being blown over.

I checked the doors on one of the hangars and found them locked, but doors on the second one rolled open easily. There was nothing in the hangar and the lack of any tracks on the dirt floor indicated that it hadn't been used for some time. With weather like this, it wasn't likely that the owner would be returning and need to use it, so I shoved the doors open and pushed the Cub inside. Just as a precaution in case the owner should return and want my ship out, I wrote a note which said, "Pilot of this ship will be at the hotel in town until the weather improves." I placed the note on the rear seat cushion, picked up my backpack and closed the hangar doors.

Not a single car passed me as I trudged along the road toward town. A hundred yards or so west of the airport fence was a vacant house with a large barn behind it. The front door stood open and some of the windows were broken, but at least it would be dry inside. I considered stopping there to get out of the drizzle which was rapidly turning into light rain but decided that since I was already rather damp, I might as well go on to town where there would be a restaurant with food and hot coffee. It was now a little past two in the afternoon and had been a long time since breakfast.

CHAPTER SIX

Backed up against the railroad tracks running parallel to main street stood a metal covered grain elevator where farmers brought their wheat to be shipped by rail to the markets. I could hear machinery running inside as it lifted grain from one bin and dumped it into another. Dust boiled from the open windows of the head tower but disappeared the instant that it came in contact with the rain. A man stood inside the big doors where trucks enter to be dumped. I waved at him and he returned the greeting.

Just past the elevator was the Case Tractor dealer. Cast iron eagles perched atop globes guarded either side of the driveway. A few pieces of nondescript farm equipment were parked around the shop building and I could hear the sound of a hammer pounding against steel coming from inside. A neon sign hanging on the front of the building flashed and flickered as raindrops spattered on open electrical connections.

Across the street from the tractor place was a squat brick building with "Studebaker" painted in big letters above the dirty windows. Several old model cars parked in front. They ranged from a Model A Ford to a couple vintage Studebakers with shiny new paint jobs. There was nothing there newer than about the beginning of WW-II. This must be one of those places which buys old cars and rebuilds them, I thought to myself. It's not usual to find a place which specializes in restoring antique and classic automobiles in the larger cities, but finding one in a remote place like this would be very unusual. On second thought, rural Nebraska might be a good place to go looking for old cars. While I'm not an antique car buff, I do get a kick out of looking at them, so I opened the door and walked inside.

A shiny black four door Studebaker sedan was parked to one side of the showroom floor and a blue two door on the other. Along the back wall of the showroom was a window with a sign above it indicating that it was the parts department. Through a glass window I could see two men sitting in an office. I opened the door of the sedan and the new-car smell wafted out. I was amazed at the restoration job which had been done on the car. Not only did it look like a new car, it even smelled like one.

"That's the brand new 1947 model; we just got it in yesterday," came a voice from behind me.

I was startled as I had not heard him approaching. "It's very nice. Where did it come from?" I replied, not being able to think of anything else to say.

The man stared at me and then at my backpack for a few seconds, wrinkled his brow as if he was unsure of what I was asking and replied, "From the Studebaker factory, where else."

I began to get the strangest feeling that something was very wrong because Studebaker had stopped building cars more than thirty years ago. Now here is a man telling me that this is a brand new 1947 model fresh from the factory. I turned my back to him and walked around the car, trying to gather my thoughts and figure out just what was going on. Between the car and the window was a couch with a coffee table in front of it. Laying on the table were several brochures about Studebaker and a copy of Life Magazine. I picked up the magazine and opened it to photos and an article about Mahatma Gandhi. I read the date on the cover, July 15, 1946.

"What is today's date?" I asked the man.

"August 24th," he replied.

"And the year," I asked in a measure voice.

"1946."

There was no way that I could carry on a conversation with this man and deal with what was happening to me, so I dropped the magazine back on the table and walked toward the door.

"Thanks and come again," he said as I stepped out into the rain.

There was a terrible fear deep in my gut as I walked toward the main part of town, not sure of where I was or how I had gotten there. Worse still, what was I going to be able to do about suddenly finding myself moved back 40 years in time. More important than that, how was I going to go about getting back to where I belonged. I had to go someplace where I could think and try to make sense out of this. Then a thought came to me, perhaps this whole situation is simply a continuation of a bad dream resulting from that Jalapeno and Anchovy pizza. I'm bound to wake up any minute and it will all be over.

The whole town looked like a set for a movie about the 1940s. The cars all dated to before the war and even their license tags showed the year to be 1946. As I walked along the street, trying to make heads or tails of what was happening, I smelled coffee and food. It reminded me that not only was a cold fear gnawing at me, but also hunger. The aroma was coming from the door to the City Cafe. It seems that there is a City Cafe in every small town, as if trying to encourage the town to grow to the status of a city.

Inside, it was warm and dry. Several varnished plywood booths lined one wall and half a dozen tables with chrome legs and formica tops were carefully lined up down the middle of the place. A long counter began at a display case filled with cigars, candy and gum and extended to near the swinging doors to the kitchen. Along the counter was a row of round chrome stools with red imitation leather cushions. Occupying the last stool next to the kitchen, a lone man who cuddled a cup of coffee with both hands.

The waitress behind the counter gave me a smile and a questioning look as she held up a coffee cup.

"Please," I said as I placed my backpack on the seat of one of the booths and slid in beside it. It was almost as if I was trying to build a barrier around myself.

The leggy waitress, who appeared to be somewhere around forty, wore her dark hair in a Betty Grable style. She had an unusually trim figure for a woman of her age and had retained the greater part of her youthful beauty. In fact, she was a strikingly beautiful lady. She placed a glass of water and a cup of steaming black coffee in front of me and asked, "Cream?"

"No, thanks, I drink it black, but you can bring me a menu."

She handed me a plastic covered menu written in pencil. Under the heading of "Plate Lunches" it listed Roast Beef, Roast Pork, Fried Chicken, Pork Chops, Corned Beef and Cabbage, Liver and Onions, Salmon Cakes and Beef Stew.

"I'll have the roast beef," I told her.

"We're out of that," she replied.

"OK, then, just bring me the roast pork."

"Out of that too. They are having court today and we had a lot of people for lunch."

I moved my finger down to the fried chicken. "No fried chicken or pork chops either," she said before I could ask. Then she added, "He didn't cook any corned beef and cabbage or liver and onions today. No body ever eats them anyway."

"Why don't you just tell me what you do have and we'll go from that," I told her.

"Salmon cakes or a hamburger is about all that's left."

"How are the salmon cakes?" I asked.

"Well, I ate them and I'm still alive," she replied with a laugh.

"I suppose that is as good a recommendation as I could ask for," I replied as I handed her the menu.

"Salmon cakes!" she shouted in the direction of the kitchen. "Match you for the music," she said as she pulled a coin from the pocket of her apron.

"I got out a quarter. We tossed the coins in the air and caught them as they came down. Both of us slapped the coins on the table. We both had heads. "Better luck next time," she said as she picked up my quarter and walked to the jute against the back wall. There was a noticeable swing to her hips as she walked.

She dropped in the coin and punched a button. An arm swung out with a record, the turntable rose and the jute box began playing a Glenn Miller recording. I finally recognized the name of the music, it was "in The Mood." Music straight out of World War Two, I thought. She swayed her hips in time with the music while she selected four more records. That kind of music coming from a jute box seemed so out of place.

"Hey Maggie, how come you don't never play nothing but that old horn music? Why don't you play something good?" asked the man at the counter.

She ignored him and returned to stand next to the booth, swinging her hips with the music. "I haven't seen you in here before, where you from?" she asked.

"Colorado," I replied in an effort to bring the conversation to an end so I could think about my situation.

"I have a sister in Denver, Ida Barnes. She works for the government at the mint. Maybe you know her?"

"I'm afraid not. I live in Black Forest.

"I grew up in Denver but I never heard of a place by that name, Where is it?"

"It's near the Air Force Academy....it's close to Colorado Springs," I corrected myself, realizing that there no such thing as an Air Force Academy in 1946. In fact, there wasn't even a branch of service called the Air Force.

"Pick up!" shouted the cook as he set my lunch in the window. As the waitress went to get it, two men came in and sat at the counter. Perhaps she would leave me alone and let me think.

She refilled my coffee cup as she set the plate on the table, then poured coffee for the two men at the counter without asking. Obviously they are regulars, I thought to myself as I surveyed my lunch. Greasy fried salmon cakes, mashed potatoes with brown gravy, pinto beans and corn. Not a single green vegetable or salad, just saturated fat and starch. This must be the cardiac arrest center of the world. No wonder that the life expectancy was ten years less in 1946 than it is only forty years later.

A thought came to me as I ate my lunch. If I had actually gone back 40 years in time, could it be that I regressed in age at the same time and I am now forty years younger. Just think of the possibilities that would offer. Seventeen years old and with the knowledge of what was going to happen during the next forty years. I looked at my hands and they appeared no different from what I remembered. I had to see what I looked like. There was a cigarette machine with a mirror next to the front door so I strolled over to it and looked into the mirror. The same face that I had shaved that morning stared back at me.

"Need some cigarette change?" asked the waitress.

"No, thanks. Just checking something," I replied.

"You look pretty good to me," she said.

It does great things for a man's ego to have a woman try to hit on him, especially one who is attractive as this one. However, that was the last thing that I needed at a time like this. "Thanks," I replied.

Suddenly a thought struck me. I have been presented with a rare opportunity. My father had been dead for thirty years and my mother twenty. This might be my chance to see them again, or at least talk with them. I finished my meal and went to the cash register to pay for it.

"That'll be sixty-five cents," said the waitress.

One thing that could be said for being back in 1946 was that it didn't cost very much to eat. I pulled a handful of quarters from my pocket and pushed five of them across the counter to her, "Keep the change, and could you tell me where I could make a long distance phone call."

"The switchboard is at the other end of this block and across the street," she replied as she put three of the quarters in the register and dropped a dime and the other two into her pocket. I swung my backpack over my shoulder and headed out the door.

The telephone office was in what had once been the living room of a home. There was a curtain hanging across the hallway leading to the back part of the house. The lady who ran it sat on a high stool in front of one of those old switchboards with a multitude of little holes and the cords which were pulled up from the base to be plugged in to complete a connection.

"I'd like to place a long distance call to the Mills Foreman residence in Stinnett, Texas," I told her.

"Do you have the number?" she asked.

"I'm sorry, but I don't remember it," I replied.

She wrote my dad's name and Stinnett on a small piece of paper, pulled up a cord, plugged it into one of the holes and pressed a lever forward with one hand while she spun a crank with the other. A few seconds later, she said, "Routing to Stinnett, Texas, please."

My palms grew sweaty. What would I say to them when they answered? What would they think when a 57 year old man called to tell them that he was their son. In 1946, they weren't even as old as I am now. I heard her ask for the Mills Foreman residence. I was just about ready to tell her to forget the call when she said, "I'm sorry, but there is no answer."

Things were getting more complicated all the time. I couldn't call my parents and what about my own wife. For all that my she knew, I was on my way to Oshkosh and was supposed to be back home in about three days. What would happen when I didn't show up with the Cub. I hadn't filed a flight plan but John knew that I was on my way and would notify the FAA if I didn't call or arrive tomorrow. The CAP would search along the route that I would have taken, but how could they find me if I had somehow slipped back in time to 1946.

I thought about it for a moment and decided to see if it was 1946 everywhere, or just where I was. "I'd like to place another call," I told her. "Please call Area Code 303, 495-2392."

"Where's that? I never heard of a number like that before." she said.

"Forget it," I replied as I walked out the door.

The rain had stopped when I came out of the telephone office so I began to walk along the sidewalk toward the west side of town to do some serious thinking. I had to try to figure out how this had happened to me and how to get back out of it. I passed the school and had turned around to walk back when I heard the bell ring inside the building. A few seconds later, a couple hundred kids of all ages came boiling out the doors. Some climbed onto waiting school busses while the others scattered for their homes in town. After the kids had gone, the teachers came out, got in their cars and left. It makes no difference whether it is 1946 or 1986, school hasn't changed a bit.

I entered the drugstore which was next to the bank. There was a rack of comic books along the wall next to the door and a sign above it read, "Buy First, Read Later" but it seemed to have no effect on the three boys who were sitting on the base of the rack, totally engrossed in the latest comics. As I hoisted myself onto one of the wrought iron stools and ran my hand over the polished marble surface of the soda fountain, a man in a white coat emerged from an alcove lined with narrow shelves of bottles of various medicines.

"What'll you have?" he asked.

"Coke," I replied.

He picked up a glass, squirted a shot and a half of dark syrup from one of the half-dozen pumps which lined the counter and reached for the ice scoop. "Make that a Coke float," I said. "I haven't had one of those in years."

He gave me a strange look as he slid the glass under one of three tall spigots. He pulled the lever toward him and filled the glass nearly full of carbonated water. He gave the coke a few quick turns with a long spoon, dropped in a scoop of vanilla ice cream and slid it across the counter to me.

He gave me a questioning look as he picked up one of the four quarters that I placed on the counter and went over to the cash register. As he rang up fifteen cents, he noticed the boys who were reading the comic books.

"If you kids can read those comic books, then you ought to be able to read that sign," he shouted.

The boys dropped the comic books like they were hot and scampered out the door.

"Damn kids," he said as he slid a dime across the marble counter to me. "If they want to read for free, they ought to go down to the library."

I took a sip the coke, which seemed to be a lot sweeter than normal, then I remembered seeing him give it an extra half shot of syrup. I guess that is his way or rewarding adults who come into his place to buy something instead of reading his comic books for free. He dumped the ice and water from some dirty glasses, swished them around in a sink filled with suds, dunked them in the rinse water and turned them upside down on a towel to drain.

"Ain't seen you around here before," he said. "You new in town or just coming through?"

"Just passing through," I replied as a woman entered with a slip of paper in her hand.

"Afternoon, Mrs. Jones," said the druggist as the door bumped shut behind her.

"Doc Pritchard give me this 'scription," she said as she handed him the slip of paper. He was reading what was written on it as he entered the small pharmacy area.

He selected one of the brown bottles from a shelf and transferred some of the pills into a smaller bottle. "I see that the doctor has changed your medicine," he said.

"Yeah, I been doin' poorly on the other medicine," she replied. "Edgar takes some of it now and then and it seems to help him more than it does me."

"How did your mother do on the medicine that I gave you?" he asked.

"She complains all the time about something so I don't know whether it helped or not," she answered.

The scintillating conversation continued as I finished the coke and pocketed my change. I doubt that the druggist even noticed me as I left. Neither had he noticed that two more boys had taken up residence at the comic book display.

When I emerged from the drugstore, the overcast seemed to have lifted slightly and I could now see at least a mile. It was just a little past four in the afternoon and darkness was still a few hours away. If I could get back into the air, I could make several miles before dark, but where would I go. No matter, I had to go someplace and do something. I couldn't sit where I was and let what was happening to me continue.

I walked to the corner and took one last look at the City Cafe before crossing the street. I could see several people milling around inside the place, business must have picked up.

CHAPTER SEVEN

I crossed the intersection and just as I passed in front of the bank, I heard footsteps behind me. A hand grabbed my shoulder, spun me toward the brick building and shoved me against it. I raised my hands to catch myself and keep my face from hitting the wall. A voice behind me commanded, "This is the law. Don't you move."

With a hand in the middle of my back shoving me against the wall, he kicked my feet apart and away from the wall until I was leaning at a forty-five degree angle. Hands felt around my waist and down my legs. My backpack was stripped off as my arms were jerked behind me and I felt handcuffs being ratcheted shut around my wrists. I was then allowed to turn around to see who was behind me. One man was short, fat and fifty. He had red hair and a red face. His belly bulged out over his belt. He was dressed in khaki pants and shirt, and wore a western hat. On his chest was a large gold star, bearing the word, Sheriff. Behind him was a rather skinny kid with lots of pimples. He looked barely old enough to vote. He was dressed in the same manner as the sheriff except that he wore a silver star. Both of the men wore pistols in leather holsters.

"What is going on here, Sheriff?" I asked.

"I'll ask the questions," he replied as he propelled me along the sidewalk beside the bank. I was helpless to do anything except to go where they wanted because the sheriff had a firm grip on one of my arms and the deputy had the other. They guided me toward the front of the courthouse. It was a depressing gray brick building of a design which could best be described as early courthouse, or a mixture of just about every type of architecture known to man. There is a saying that if a committee set out to design a horse, they would come up with a camel. It also seems that this same committee designed most courthouses. With the tall, narrow windows, the basic building could be called modern. However, those lines were ruined by the Gothic towers on each corner. Sticking out from the front of the building was a huge Greek arch supported by four tall columns. It looked like something added as an afterthought. Engraved across the front of the arch was HVLSEY COVNTY COVRT HOVSE. For the life of me, I have never been able to see any reason why people who design courthouses insist on using the letter V instead of a U. Perhaps they feel that this makes the building seem more judicial or something.

A small replica of the statue of liberty stood to the right of the sidewalk leading to the building and an old field cannon which dated to somewhere around World War One sat on a concrete slab on the other. The wheels on the cannon were secured in place by a large chain which emerged from the concrete, ran between the spokes and back into the slab. Evidently someone had done this as a precaution to keep kids rolling it away.

They propelled me along the sidewalk toward the front of the courthouse, but instead of taking me up the steps and between the tall columns, they guided me around to one side of the portico, down a half-flight of steps which led under it and through a door leading into the basement. The sheriff inserted a key in the lock of a thick oak door and swung it open. Inside was a huge roll top desk with an oak chair with arms on it. There was a stout oak table with a chair on either side. Along one end of the room, iron bars and a steel door enclosed a small cell which contained nothing except a white toilet bowl without a seat and an iron cot with a bare cotton mattress. The whole place reeked of Pine Sol and stale cigarettes. This was obviously the room where the sheriff interrogated prisoners and its location suggested that he could interrogate as vigorously as he wished without anyone hearing what was going on. I suddenly remembered stories about confessions which had been extracted by the enthusiastic use of a rubber hose.

The sheriff closed the door, removed the handcuffs and told me to empty my pockets onto a table. I had a pocket knife, a comb, a ring of keys, some nail clippers and about twelve dollars in change, mostly quarters, in my pants pockets, as well as a handkerchief and my wallet in my back pockets. I put them on the table.

The sheriff sorted through the things which I had removed from my pockets then he opened my backpack and began to dig through it. He pulled out my shaving kit followed by a pair of pants, two shirts, three pairs of socks and three changes of underwear. After inspecting each item, he placed it on the table. Then he opened my shaving kit and went through the contents. One of the items which seemed to interest him the most was a plastic disposable razor. The last thing that he looked at was my portable radio. He turned it over in his hands, looked at the knobs and read the FCC notice on the back. "What is this?" he asked.

"That's a radio, Sheriff."

"Little thing like this can't pick up much," he said. "How does it work?"

I reached over and took it from his hand and turned it on. I knew that there wasn't a chance that anyone was going to hear it in 1946 because they did start using VHF frequencies for civilian aviation until around 1950. However, since the military did earlier, I thought that there might be a chance that some military pilot would hear me and respond. I switched it to 121.5, the universal emergency frequency, and pressed the talk button. The red transmit light came on and a small beep came from the speaker. I continued to hold it down as I talked. "It's used just for emergencies. If I simply said Mayday, Mayday into it, everyone would know that I had an emergency here in Sanger, Nebraska."

"What the hell are you doing?" shouted the sheriff as he snatched it away.

"Just trying to get some music for you," I replied. "But I guess that we are too far from a station.

He turned it off and laid it on top of my clothing.

"Would you please tell me what you are holding me for," I asked.

"I'm sure that you know why you are here. You may think that just because this is a small town, all of the people in it are stupid," he replied as he dug through my wallet.

"Well, I certainly haven't done anything wrong and know of no reason why you should cuff and search me. I want you to either tell me what your probable cause is for arresting me or else release me," I told him.

"What do you mean by probable cause? Are you a smart-asked lawyer or something, Mister Foreman?" he said as he read my name from my drivers license.

"No, I'm not a lawyer, but probable cause means that an officer has to have a good and valid reason for stopping a person, much less detaining him under arrest. I take it that since you placed handcuffs on me and brought me here, I am under arrest," I replied.

"You're damn sure right that you're under arrest and I have a damn good cause for doing it."

"What is that cause?"

"Passing counterfeit money is a good enough cause for a starter. No telling what else I can hold you for once we get into it," said the sheriff.

"That's crazy. I'm no counterfeiter. What gave you an idea like that?"

"It doesn't take a genius to figure that out. You have a whole pocket full of counterfeit quarters on you. You passed three of them over at the cafe and gave two more to the waitress. She also said that you gave her one which she put into the jute box. Anyone with any sense at all can see the copper showing through the edge of these coins and know that they are slugs. Not only are they easy to spot with the copper insides showing, but they even have the wrong dates on them. Look at this one, it is dated 1982. Everyone knows that this is 1946."

He opened my wallet and pulled out the money. He looked at the new twenty dollar bills and let out a low whistle as he counted them. "This guy has over five hundred dollars on him," he told his deputy. "Melvin, go around to the bank and get Lester Bales to come in here and have a look at all these counterfeit twenties."

"What do these keys fit?" asked the sheriff as he inspected each key on the ring.

"My car, my pickup and my house," I answered.

He paid particular attention to the key with the plastic covered head. He read the name on it and asked, "What's a Mazda."

"That's the key to my pickup truck, it's a Mazda," I replied.

"Don't get smart with me fellow, I happen to know that there's no such make of pickup. Now, I'm asking you once more to tell me what this key fits."

I knew that the answer wasn't going to satisfy him but couldn't think of anything else to say at the moment, "It fits a Mazda pickup which is made in Japan."

"I don't know what's going on here, but I can tell you one thing for damn sure. If this key fits a pickup which was made in Japan, then you are in a whole lot more trouble than you think. Those little yellow bellied bastards killed my only son and both of Melvin's brothers, so you'd better come up with some good answers in a hurry."

Before the conversation could go any further, the deputy returned with a little man who was wearing round glasses and one of those green eyeshades that looks like the bill on a baseball cap. He looked at the bills, felt the paper and rubbed them with his thumb. He finally said, "Sheriff, I never saw any bills like these before, counterfeit or otherwise. These bills are called Federal Reserve Notes, not Silver Certificates like all the other twenties that I've ever seen. I never heard of such a bill and look at the dates on them. However, I'd swear that the paper and printing is authentic. I wouldn't take one at the bank, but on the other hand, I wouldn't say that they are counterfeit either. If they are bogus, they are the best ones that I've ever seen."

Then Bales and the sheriff began to look at my credit cards. They read what was printed on them, felt the embossed numbers and ran their fingers over the magnetic strip on the back. "What are these?" asked the sheriff.

"Credit cards," I answered, trying not to open up any unnecessary areas for more questions.

"I recognize the names of Phillips, Mobil and Texaco, but these other cards say that they were issued by banks. I never heard of anything called Visa, MasterCard or Discover, what are they for?" asked Bales.

"They are also credit cards," I replied.

"Credit cards for what?" he asked.

"Where I come from, Mister Bales, a person can use those cards to charge merchandise at just about any store or they can use them to draw cash at a bank."

"How are they used?" he asked.

I wasn't about to try to explain about automatic tellers, so I told him, "You give the card to a teller and tell him how much money you want. He will use the card to stamp a form, you sign your name and he gives you the cash."

"How much money can you get on a card like this," he asked, holding up my Discover card.

"My credit limit on that card is five thousand dollars," I replied.

"And these," he said, holding up the Visa and MasterCard.

"I believe that the limit on them is the same as the Discover card," I answered.

"You mean to say that you can take these three cards into a bank and get fifteen thousand dollars in cash, just like that, no notes, no mortgages or anything," he asked.

"That's right, and the Discover card is also good at any Sears store."

"You carry over five hundred dollars in cash in your pocket and claim that you can get another fifteen thousand dollars just by handing these cards to a bank, I don't believe it. Hells Fire, Mister J. D. Rockefeller couldn't even do that," said Bales.

"And I don't believe it either. This guy has to be either the smartest man on earth or else the dumbest," said the sheriff. "Thanks for the help, Lester. You can go on back to the bank."

The sheriff picked up my drivers license, looked at my photo on it and asked, "When were you born?"

November Third, 1928," I replied.

He counted up on his fingers and said, "That would make you seventeen years old. Hell, you look older than I am."

"I probably am. Look at the date the license was issued."

The sheriff wrote my name on a small blackboard with chalk, handed it to me to hold and told me to stand against the wall. Painted on the wall were marks and numbers indicating height. He got out a brownie camera, inserted a bulb in the flash and snapped my photo. "Now turn sideways," he said, then he snapped another from that view.

He cranked the rest of the film through the camera, removed the roll and handed it to the deputy. "Take this down to the drug store and tell them that I need three prints of each one and that I need them back as quick as possible."

By the time that the sheriff had finished finger printing me, the deputy had returned. "The pictures will be back in about a week," he said.

I doubted that the sheriff was going to buy any story about my being from someplace 40 years in his future, but I had to try something. "Sheriff, I know that you are going to find this awfully hard to believe, but I am actually from the year 1986. Strictly by some sort of accident, I am trapped here in 1946. The credit cards, money and everything else that you see there is authentic."

I should have known that this question would be the next one as the sheriff asked, "You say that you are from 1986, then tell me how in hell did you get back here?"

I didn't know myself how I had gotten there and it was going to be even harder trying to come up with something that the sheriff might believe. Before I could answer, Melvin saved the day, "I'll bet that he's one of them alien things and came in on that flying saucer that I was chasing last night!"

"You know, Sheriff, your deputy is a lot smarter than you'd think. He is absolutely right, I came on that flying saucer, only we don't call them that. We have had both space and time travel for several years and that's how I came here. I was away from the ship last night when your deputy almost discovered us and they had to move without me."

"See, I told you that I almost caught that flying saucer. I got real close and all of a sudden, Zoom! it was gone. How does it go that fast? " Melvin asked excitedly.

"It didn't actually go anywhere, it simply stayed where it was and moved into another time element."

"What do you mean another time element?" asked the sheriff.

This story was going a lot better than I had expected. Perhaps I could convince this man to let me go and I could try to work myself out of this mess. "I'll use a very simple example to show you how I got to this point in time. Suppose that you arrived in front of the bank at exactly ten in the morning and saw a car drive by. Had that car driven been going twice as fast from the time he left home until he passed in front of the bank, would you have seen it?

"Why, hell no I wouldn't because he had already gone by."

"Correct, and suppose that he had been driving only half as fast and you left the bank at ten, would have been there to see it when it did come by."

"I still don't see what you are talking about," said the sheriff.

"That's the way that time travel works. Melvin could no longer see the ship because it was no longer there at the time when he was looking."

"Sounds like a bunch of Buck Rogers stuff to me. What were you doing here?" asked the sheriff.

"Agricultural research," I replied. "We were taking soil samples to see what changes in mineral content have taken place over the past 40 years and how they have effected crop production. With that knowledge, we will be able to predict what will happen to food production in this area in years to come."

"Was anyone else left here except you?"

"No, I was the only one."

"How are you going to get back?"

"No problem, they know where I am and the precise time element when I was left. They will be back after me. Leaving someone on the ground is not unusual. Occasionally, people will be left in a time element for an extended length of time for one reason or another. We prepare people who will remain in another time element but in my case we didn't anticipate Melvin nearly catching the ship on the ground. If they had, I would have had money and papers from this time element so something like this wouldn't happen. I didn't think anyone would notice if I spent nothing but coins."

"What does the flying saucer look like?" asked Melvin.

I started to tell him that it was round with windows but remembered my watch. I raised my sleeve and showed them the picture of the Space Shuttle. "This is what it looks like."

"That doesn't look like what I saw last night. It was more like a bowl or hubcap," said Melvin.

"You were probably seeing it from the front," I replied. It would look something like what you describe, especially when seen in the dark."

"What does NASA stand for?" asked the sheriff.

"NASA stand for National Agricultural Science Administration. I work for them," I replied, figuring that he could understand agriculture and science better than space.

"Wow, that is some watch. Look at all the buttons," said Melvin. "How does it work?"

"It's an atomic powered watch which will run for at least a thousand years. NASA furnishes them to all of their employees who time travel. With an atomic watch, we can adjust time to a millionth of a second."

"It doesn't have any hands, just numbers, and keeps flashing back and forth. What does TH-8-24-86 mean?" he asked.

"That means that today is Thursday, August 24th, 1986, or at least it is 1986 in the time element where I come from."

The sheriff pulled out a large gold pocket watch and compared the time on it against my watch. "It doesn't keep very good time, it's an hour fast," he said.

"The watch is set for Daylight Savings Time, or what you called War Time. Let me correct it," I said as I changed it back to standard time. The watch instantly switched to the correct time.

"Wow!" said Melvin as he looked at the watch. "You didn't have to turn a knob or do anything except press a button and it changed just like that."

"What are all those other buttons for?" asked the sheriff.

"In addition to being a watch, it is an electronic calculator which will do all of the normal mathematical functions plus a lot more."

"When are you supposed to be picked up and how will they find you?" asked the sheriff.

I could see where he was going so I thought that I'd give him a reason for letting me go. "I don't know the exact time that they will be here to pick me up but I assure you that they not only know where I am at this moment but that I'm behind held prisoner. That means that they will send their forced recovery team to get me."

"What's a forced recovery team?" asked Melvin.

"That is part of the security force on the ship and they are trained to use whatever force is necessary to recover one of their people."

"They'd have to go past me if you're in my jail," said the sheriff as he patted the pistol on his hip.

"Sheriff, if we have the technology to build time travel shuttles and atomic watches, do you think that mere guns or jail bars would pose the slightest problem to the recovery team? Remember the atomic bombs we used on Japan, well today those are as obsolete as firecrackers. The recovery team tries to avoid direct conflict in another time element if at all possible, but as I said, they come prepared to use whatever force necessary to complete their mission. So, why don't you release me and avoid placing you and your deputy in jeopardy. When I walk out that door, you will never see me again."

He sat there and thought about what I had said for several minutes. "I've been a sheriff for twenty years and I've heard all sorts of stories, but I have never heard such a bunch of bullshit in all my days. I'm not about to let you walk out of here and since this involves counterfeiting, I'm going to turn this over to the FBI and the Treasury Department."

He gave the phone a crank, picked it and said, "Lillie, this is the Sheriff. Get me the FBI in Omaha."

Damn, if the FBI get involved in this, I might never get out. I have to get away from this place some way, but how.

After telling the FBI what he knew about me, he hung up the phone and said, "The FBI will be here to pick you tomorrow. In the meantime, you are going to be a guest of Hulsey County."

"Want me to take him up stairs and book him?" asked Melvin.

"No, we'll keep him down here in the holding cell. The FBI said that since he claims to have come in a flying saucer, this might be something top secret and they don't want him to see or talk to anyone until they have a chance to interrogate him."

"Sheriff, under the Miranda Decision, I have the right to an attorney and I want to see one right now."

"You don't have any rights of any kind while you are in my jail unless I say so. I'll decide if and when you can see a lawyer, and what the hell is all this bull about a Miranda Decision anyway?"

It suddenly occurred to me that the Miranda Decision didn't come down until a number of years after 1946. "I forgot that the Miranda case wasn't heard by the Supreme Court until several years from now, so it's not surprising that you haven't heard of it."

"You seem to know all this legal stuff, just what is this decision that you are talking about?" he asked.

"The Supreme Court issued a decision in a landmark case concerning a man by the name of Miranda and that is why it is called the Miranda Decision. They ruled that if a person is placed under arrest, the arresting officer must inform him of his constitutional rights. He has to inform the prisoner that he has the right to remain silent and that anything that he says can be used against him in a court or law. He also has the right to have an attorney present while he is being questioned and if he can't afford an attorney, one has to be provided for him."

"Bullshit! The Supreme Court would never do such a thing to the law officers of the nation. That would tie their hands and the criminals would take over. Lock him up Melvin, and you stay here with him, I'm going home to get something to eat. I'll have the cafe send something over for you and him."

CHAPTER EIGHT

There was a knock on the door and Melvin got up and opened it. The waitress who I had seen earlier at the cafe brought in a tray with two plates of food and two cups of coffee on it. "I figured that since you had salmon cakes for lunch, you might like something different tonight, so I brought you some nice pork chops," she said as she went to the table and set the tray down beside my belongings.

"Thanks, it looks good," I replied.

She turned to look at me. "I thought that there was something odd about you when you came in with that ditty-bag on your back. At first, I figured that you were just a bum off the train who wanted a free meal, but when you paid for it and gave me a big tip, I knew that something about you was suspicious. Nobody ever leaves a half dollar tip for a plate lunch, at least not around here. After you left, I took a good look at the quarters and saw that they were slugs, so I showed them to the boss. He is the one who called the sheriff and had you arrested. Sorry if I caused you a peck of trouble, but you not only stiffed me on the tip, the boss made me pay for your meal too."

"I'm sorry miss, but I never intended to do you any harm. The truth is that those quarters are as good as gold, but there has been a mistake all around about them."

Melvin broke in, "You'll have to go now Maggie, 'cause the sheriff said that this guy came in on a flying saucer and no one can talk to him until the FBI gets here tomorrow."

Melvin closed and locked the door as she left. He turned to me and said, "If I let you out to eat, will you promise not to try to escape or anything?"

"I promise and can assure you that I won't do anything which might cause me even more trouble than I already have. I'm innocent and this whole thing will be straightened out once the FBI gets here. I know enough about the law to know that if I try to escape while I'm in your custody, it would become a crime."

Melvin unlocked the cell door and we sat down to eat our dinners. "Would you let me look at your watch?" he asked.

I took it off and handed it to him. He held it to his ear for a moment and said, "It isn't running."

"Yes it is, it just doesn't make any sound, at least no sound that a human can hear. Look at the dial, see it changing back and forth between the time and date."

"Show me how it works," he said.

"This watch will do lots of things. First of all, it will tell you the time and date anywhere in the world. Take for instance, if you want to know what time it is in New York, you press the time zone button, then key in NY. Watch it change." It changed instantly from 8:23 PM to 9:23 PM. Now watch what happens when I change it to Tokyo, not only the time changes, but also the date since Tokyo is a day ahead of us.

"That's amazing, how does it know what time it is in all those places?"

"Telling time is simple," I replied. "Let me show you a few other things that it will do. Suppose that you want to multiply a number like 257864 times 71. Just put them in and press the equals button and you have the answer, 18308344."

"How much does a watch like that cost?" he asked.

"The government furnishes them to us, so they probably cost a lot more than most people could afford. However, considering that it will run for three or four thousand years, I suppose that the cost doesn't really matter."

"What is it like living in 1986?" he asked.

"Pretty much the same as it is now. We live in the same kinds of houses as you do, eat basically the same foods and work for a living. After all, it is only forty years later. Think how little things have changed between 1906 and now. We earn a lot more money but it also costs a lot more to live."

"But you have atomic watches like that and are able to travel through time."

"True, we have made a number of advances in technology, but there has been very little change in the human body or mind. It hasn't changed much in the past millions years, so it couldn't have changed very much in another forty," I told him. "We still fall in love, get married and have kids. We get old, get sick and die just like you do now."

"I joined the Navy after my brothers were killed but since I was the only son left in the family, they kept me in the states until the war was over. I had served just a little over a year before the war ended and they discharged me. Has there been another war or anything like that?" he asked.

"I'm afraid that is one field in which we haven't made much progress. There will be in another war in 1950 in a place called Korea but you probably won't have to go back in since you served more than a year during World War Two. The Korean war will last for about three years and will end with neither side winning."

"You know all sorts of things that will happen in the future. You must know who will win things like the World Series and the Kentucky Derby. If you told me, I could bet on them and make a lot of money."

"I don't remember who won those things, but I can give you a few tips that will make you a rich man. Do you have any money to invest?"

"I have twenty thousand dollars drawing three percent interest at the bank. It's the money I got from GI Insurance when my brothers were killed in the war, but I've been saving that to buy me a good farm with," Melvin replied.

"I hate to tell you this, but buying a farm in this area wouldn't be the way to make money. You would probably be able to make a comfortable living off it for a number of years, but you stand a good chance of losing it just about the time when you are old enough to think about retiring."

"If I owned a farm outright, how would I be likely to lose it?" asked Melvin.

"As time goes along, the agricultural market will become so unstable that you will have to borrow money just to keep going. Each year you will have to borrow more than you will be able to pay back until you reach a point where you will owe more than the farm is worth and then the bankers will take it over. It's a sad fact that bankers are the most insistent about getting their money just when you are the least able to repay it. Over half of the farmers in this area will go broke and lose their farms during the next forty years."

"Then what should I do?" he asked.

"If you really want to make some money, take that twenty thousand dollars and buy every share of stock that you can in three companies. They are called Polaroid, IBM and XEROX. Don't cash in any of the stock no matter how much you think that you need the money. When you get dividend checks, use that money to buy more shares of stock. By the time that you are forty years old, you will be a millionaire. In the meantime, use your GI Bill to get yourself a college education."

"If I went to college, I'd have to quit this job," he replied.

"Jobs like you have now will be a dime a dozen. The job that you will be doing ten years from now probably doesn't even exist today."

"I've never heard of any companies by those names, what are they?"

"I don't think that any of them exist yet. Polaroid will make cameras which will produce a finished print in only one minute after you take the picture."

"You say they will give you a picture in a minute, without having to take the film to the drug store."

"That's right. You snap the picture, wait a minute and pull out a finished photograph. After they have been in business a few years, they will start making a camera which will produce a color photograph in just one minute."

"That sounds amazing. No wonder that their stock will go up and up," he replied. "But what about those other two companies that you told me about. What will they make?"

"IBM will build a number of different kinds of business machines, but computers will be the thing which will make the most money for them and XEROX will make copying machines."

"Do you mean photostat machines, like the one which they have in the County Clerk's office?" he asked.

"XEROX Copiers will do basically the same thing that photostat machines do now, except that it will produce an exact copy in a few seconds. The cost of a XEROX copy will be about two cents as compared to a couple dollars for a photostat."

"If these companies don't exist now, then how am I going to buy stock in them?"

"Keep in touch with some stock broker and the day that stock in these companies comes on the market, buy all that you have money for. I'd suggest that you put about a third of your money in each company, then set back and watch the value grow."

"That is awfully hard to believe," Melvin said with a shake of his head. "I'd hate to sink all of my money into stocks like that and then lose it all like my dad did in 1929. At one time, he had a lot of money but when he died in 1937 he was so broke that the county had to bury him."

"Melvin, stocks will go up and down over the next few years, but I can assure you that there will not be another market crash like the one in 1929. Stock in those three companies will do nothing but go up in value."

Melvin wrote down the names of the companies and thought about what I had said for a long time before he asked, "Those people that will come after you. Will they have guns or do they use death rays and things like that?"

I couldn't tell if I had gotten to the sheriff or not, but evidently Melvin had taken it all in and was concerned about what was going to happen when they came to rescue me. "They don't use death rays any more, they use stun rays. When they zap you with a stun ray, you remain conscious but you can't move. It's extremely painful and lasts for about eight hours, but it doesn't kill a person."

"Can they knock down doors and things like that with those rays?"

"No, stun rays will go right through doors or walls and are used only against people. When the team comes, they will scan the room to find out who is in it and where they are, then there will be a flash of light and everyone except me will be instantly stunned. After that, they will use a disintegrator ray to take out locks, doors or anything else which is in their way. Normally, they never use a disintegrator ray against a person because the only thing left would be a cloud of very bad smelling smoke."

"Sounds like we won't have much of a chance," he said.

I could see that I had him going and that he was scared. Now if I could only push him into letting me go. "I guarantee that you will have absolutely no chance at all. The team is very professional and will do whatever is necessary to accomplish their mission. They don't really want to hurt or kill anyone, but they are ready if it comes to that. I'd hate to see you go through the pain of being stunned but it will happen before you even know that the team is here."

"When do you think that they will come?" Melvin asked.

"They will be here tonight because they already know where I am and that I'm in trouble. We won't know that they are around until it's too late to do anything about them. You will just be sitting there and suddenly you will have been stunned."

~How do they know exactly where you are?" he asked.

"Simple. You remember when I had the communicator for a few seconds. I switched to emergency location frequency and pressed the button. I didn't have to say anything because the sensors in the ship instantly locked in on it. I know the sheriff is rather old fashioned and dedicated to his job, but you are young and can look at things in an intelligent manner. You realize the futility of trying to hold me after the team comes, so why don't you let me gather my things and walk out that door. You can tell the sheriff that the team came and you were stunned and couldn't do anything to stop them."

"I know that I can't stop them when they get here, but I took an oath when I became a deputy and it is my sworn duty to hold you as long as I can. I just can't let you walk out," he said.

"I realize that you are a dedicated law officer, but there comes a time when you have to make decisions on your own. I like you and don't want to see you hurt, but I do have to return to 1986 where I belong. How would you like to get accidentally stuck back in 1906 or some time like that?"

"I can see your point, but I just don't know."

"To prove that I like you and care what happens to you, I'll give you that watch if you will simply let me walk away. I'm going to go anyway, so you can make it easy on yourself and have an atomic watch thirty years before anyone else."

"I'll tell you what," he said suddenly. "I'll lock the cell door but leave you out here in the office. Then I'll leave to take those dishes back to the cafe. If you aren't here when I get back, the sheriff will think that the team came and took you away while I was gone."

"OK, just give me all of the time that you can because I'm on foot and not sure just when the shuttle will come."

Melvin locked the cell door and waited while I stuffed my clothing into the back pack. "OK, you lead the way to be sure the coast is clear and I'll follow. When you head for the cafe, I'll go the other way. You don't know what a favor you are doing and how much I appreciate it."

It was dark but no longer raining when we stepped out the door beneath the front steps of the court house. I shook Melvin's hand and whispered, "Melvin, you're a good man, take care of yourself."

Behind us came the sound of a shell being jacked into a pump shotgun, then the sheriff's rough voice, "Get your hands in the air and don't either of you bastards move or I'll blow your asses to kingdom come. I knew that Melvin wasn't too smart and figured that you'd try to talk him into something stupid like this."

I felt the cold, round end of the shotgun barrel shoved against the back of my neck. "Don't you even breathe," he said as he reached around Melvin with his free hand and jerked his pistol from its holster.

"I'm not moving a muscle, sheriff, and please be careful with that shotgun. I'd hate to have my brains scattered all over the place."

"You are attempting to escape jail and I'd be justified if I pulled the trigger right now," the sheriff growled.

"You're lucky the FBI knows you are here or I'd finish you off right here. Now move real slow back down the stairs. Melvin, open the doors for us."

We walked slowly back into the sheriff's office. Melvin took the ring of keys from the top drawer of the desk and opened the cell door. The sheriff was holding Melvin's pistol in one hand and the shotgun in the other. He prodded me into the cell with the barrel of the shotgun, stepped back and said, "Slip your arms out of that knapsack real easy and push it out the door with your foot, then back up against the wall."

I did what the sheriff had ordered and he kicked the cell door shut with a loud clang. He dropped Melvin's pistol into the desk drawer, threw the keys in with it and slammed the drawer shut. Then he turned to his deputy, "Melvin, I'm real disappointed in you. If you weren't my sister's kid, you'd be in that cell too. Now give me your badge and go home, I'll decide what to do with you tomorrow."

"Don't be too hard on him Sheriff. He was just doing what he felt was best for everyone concerned," I said.

"You keep your two cents worth out of this. I ought to work you over with a sap just to teach you a little respect for me and the law. There's never been a prisoner escape from my custody before and you ain't going to tarnish my record by being the first. Several people have tried to break out of my jail before and none of them are around to brag about it today. If you weren't such an important prisoner and wanted by the FBI, you'd be a dead man right now. You better count your lucky stars that you got away with this try, but let me tell you one thing for sure, attempt to escape again and I'll kill you where you stand. You understand that?"

"Yes, Sheriff. I understand you perfectly," I replied as I sat down on the cot.

The sheriff kicked a chair against the door, plopped into it and laid the shotgun across his lap. It was obvious that he was going to stand guard over me for the rest of the night. I thought about telling him the same story that I had told Melvin, about people with stun rays coming to rescue me, but decided that might provoke him into putting me in irons or something worse. I finally decided that I would probably be better off to wait for the FBI and try to convince them that I was in 1946 as a result of some terrible mistake. At least they wouldn't be as dangerous as this man. I pulled off my shoes and laid down on the cot. The rough mattress stank of cigarettes, vomit and sweat.

Even though it was late August, there was a chilly dampness in the basement. "Any chance that I could have a blanket?" I asked the sheriff.

"Hell no you can't have a blanket. This ain't no hotel. You're costing me a night's sleep in my own bed, so you don't deserve one," he shot back. There was no chance that I could reason with a man like this, so I gained what comfort that I could from my light jacket. I finally dosed into a fitful sleep.

CHAPTER NINE

I was jolted awake by a sudden noise and as my senses gathered, I realized that the sound which roused me was someone snoring. I turned my head slowly to where I could see the sheriff. His head was leaned back against the door and flopped over to one side as if his neck was broken. His mouth hung open and a trail of saliva trickled from the lower corner and onto his shirt. His right hand was still clutching the stock of the shotgun but the barrel had slipped off his lap and the end of it was resting on the floor. He would snore lightly a few times and then jerk and give a loud snort. I wondered what time it was but Melvin had my watch. I had a travel alarm clock in my shaving kit, but it was in my backpack on the table. My bladder was full so I got up quietly to use the toilet.

As I stood there relieving myself, there was a loud pounding on the door. The sheriff leaped to his feet and as his sleep-filled eyes focused on me standing in the cell, he jerked the shotgun around toward me. "Don't you move, you bastard, or I'll blow you in two," he shouted.

Before I could answer, a voice came from outside the door, "Sheriff! Sheriff Nester! You in there?"

The sheriff lowered the shotgun, moved the chair aside and opened the door. A man thrust his head inside and said, "Thank God I found you, Sheriff. I been looking all over for you and finally woke up Melvin and he told me that you were down here guarding a prisoner. You got to get out to the Bradley place, there's been a shooting and old man Bradley is dead. They think his hired hand did it."

The sheriff looked at me and hesitated a minute. The man continued, "You better hurry, The guy who shot him is holed up in the barn and he's taking pot shots at anyone who sticks their head up."

The sheriff grabbed his hat and said to me, "You'd better be here when I get back if you know what's good for you."

"How could I go anywhere?"

I listened as the sheriff and the other man went out the door of the basement and let it slam shut behind them. In his anger at my near escape, the sheriff had forgotten to take anything away from me except my backpack and I couldn't remember his ever removing the cell keys from the desk drawer where he threw them. The desk was a good three feet from the bars of the cell and I had nothing which I could use to reach the drawer. If only I could pull the desk closer.

I pulled off my belt and on the back side of the buckle was a small hook which fastened into the holes in the belt. I stuck my arm between the bars and swung the buckle at the desk. It clanked down on the top and slid off the smooth surface. There was nothing for it to catch on. I tried a swinging motion to see if I could make the buckle go into one of the pigeon holes but it would simply bounce out. I pulled the cot aside so I could work from floor level and try to catch one of the legs of the desk. Perhaps once out of every twenty tries, the buckle would stand on edge and once out of perhaps every ten times that happened, the hook would snag the square leg. The only problem was that I had to pull at an angle and as I did so, it would slip off. I have no idea how long I tried, but it seemed as if I swung the belt a thousand times with no success.

I was really getting discouraged when I stood up to see if I could figure out any other possible way which I could snag the desk and pull it to me. I stood there looking at the cigarette burns along the edge of the desk when I noticed a small brass plate attached with two screws. It was midway of the top surface of the desk and about two inches back from the front edge. It didn't occur to me what it was for until I looked at the roll top of the desk and saw the lock mechanism sticking out of the lower rail. It was the locking plate and in the center was a small, spring-loaded cover which snapped shut when the top was rolled back. Perhaps I could catch the hook on my buckle in that hole.

I put my arm between the bars and swung the buckle at the top of the desk. It took me several tries before I got the right swing and distance to the hole. It was barely within my reach and if the hook did snag the opening, I would be able to pull only with one hand. As a safety measure in case that the belt should slip out of my hand, I took the laces out of one of my shoes, ran them through the end hole in the belt and tied the ends to my wrist. I was now able to swing the belt with one hand while holding onto the shoelace with the other.

I have no idea how man times I swung and dropped the buckle onto the desk, only to have it bounce off. I was about to give up the idea when suddenly, it hit in just the right spot and the hook dropped into the hole. I pulled lightly on the belt and could see that the hook on the back of the buckle was firmly engaged in the slot.

Using extreme care to keep the hook from coming loose, I tugged on the belt but the desk refused to move. With one hand on the belt and the other grasping the shoelace, I pulled harder; but instead of sliding toward me, the desk began to tilt up on its front two legs. If I pulled any harder, the desk would have tipped over onto the floor. I slowly allowed the desk to return to its original position, being careful not to lose my grip on the belt or the shoestring. If I ever dropped it, I would never be able to reach it again. I was glad that I had tied the shoestring to the belt so I could hang onto it with both hands. The only result of pulling at that angle would be that the desk would tip over with the drawers against the floor. If that happened, I would never be able to get at the keys.

I moved along the bars, passing the end of the belt and shoestrings from one hand to the other until I was in a position which would allow me to pull the desk endwise toward the bars. I tugged on the belt but nothing happened, the heavy desk remained where it was. I shifted around to where I could get both arms between the bars but I still couldn't reach the end of the belt with both hands. I held onto the belt with one hand and grabbed the loop of the shoelaces with the other. I tugged with all my strength, the desk gave a protesting scrape and moved a few inches toward me. I could now grasp the belt with both hands and gave it another pull, three more inches. A few more tugs and I was able to reach the end of the desk and pull it next to the bars.

The keys were in the top drawer at the opposite end of the desk and it would have to be rotated toward the bars in order for me to reach them. I pulled on the front of the desk with one hand while pushing at the back with the other. It took every ounce of my strength to make the heavy desk budge even an inch and within a few minutes, I was soaked with sweat. I wiped the sweat off my face with my handkerchief and dropped it on the bed. I had to get the desk turned to where I could reach the drawer with the keys before the sheriff returned so I kept tugging and pushing with all my might.

Inch by inch the desk swung around until I was finally able to reach the pull on the drawer with one finger and work it open. I tried to pull the drawer all the way out but it had some sort of catch which allowed it to open only about half of its length. I groped around in the drawer and my fingers touched cold metal. It was Melvin's pistol. I felt around some more and found his badge. Had the sheriff taken the keys from the drawer while I was asleep?

I stood up to where I could see down into the drawer and there were the keys, but when the sheriff threw them in, they had bounced all the way to the very back. I reached as far into the drawer as the bars would allow but the keys were still just out of my reach. I looked around for something which I could use to drag the keys toward me and finally it dawned on me that it was right in front of my eyes, Melvin's pistol. Using the front sight as a hook, I had the keys in my hand within seconds.

Since I could not see the key slot and there were three almost identical keys on the ring, it took a bit of fumbling to get the correct one inserted and turn to unlock the door. The door bumped against the desk, but after closing the drawer, I was able to squeeze out. My first thought was to get out of that place as quickly as possible but decided that I might be able to buy some time by making the sheriff wonder just how I had escaped.

I shoved the desk back to where it had been, locked the cell door and replaced the keys in the drawer. I shouldered my backpack, picked up Melvin's pistol and shoved it in my belt. As I reached for the door knob, I stopped to consider whether it would be wise to take the pistol with me or not. By taking the gun with me, I would automatically be considered as armed and dangerous. In light of what the sheriff had said about shooting jail escapees and especially if he knew that I was carrying a gun, he would probably start shooting at me on sight. I put the pistol back into the drawer and closed it.

I slipped out into the quiet hall and closed the door to the office behind me. I went to the door which we had entered when the sheriff brought me in, but just as I opened it, I heard cars driving up and saw headlights flashing across the wall above me as they pulled in to park in front of the court house. I heard car doors slam and shouting voices. With this escape route cut off, I had to find another one and in a hurry. I ran back into the basement of the court house.

The hall that I was in ran from under the stairs at the front of the building to a matching pair of large gray doors at the back. Figuring that this must lead to the back of the court house, I ran to them but they were locked. An intersecting hall led off in either direction. There were several closed doors on either side of each hall. As I frantically looked for another way out of the basement, I could hear voices approaching the front doors. Just around the corner from the room where I had been held was a green steel door. I turned the knob and it swung open. It was an elevator and that would be my escape route to a higher floor. Once out of the basement and the approaching sheriff, I could find a way to get out of the building. I stepped in and closed the door. There were only two black buttons on the control panel, one was marked BASEMENT and the other JAIL. Then it dawned on me that the only purpose of this elevator was to transport prisoners between the basement and jail on the top floor without having to go through the public part of the courthouse. If I pushed that top button, my next stop would be inside the jail upstairs.

I opened the door an inch and listened to the voices in the hall around the corner from me. There was a lot of shouting and scuffling of feet as if a struggle of some sort was going on. Directly across the hall was a gray steel door so I bolted for it. The knob turned easily, the door swung open and I leaped inside. I realized that I was now in the utility and boiler room of the court house. The room contained a huge boiler, along with the usual maintenance and janitorial equipment which one would expect find in such a place. It smelled of disinfectant, soap and floor wax.

There were only two doors in the room, other than the one which I had entered, so I tried them. One opened into a room which contained the electrical switches and fuses for the building, while the other was a storage closet filled with soap, toilet paper and large cans of floor wax. It also contained several brooms and mops, as well as a pile of rags. I didn't see anything that might be useful in my escape.

There wasn't even a window in the place and there seemed to be no other way out other than the door through which I had entered. In order to give myself a little more time in the event that the sheriff began a search of the building for me, I turned the knob which locked door to the boiler room.

I walked around the room, searching for some place where I could hide in case the sheriff should come in. Behind the boiler were the walls of an old coal bin which was used during the days before natural gas was piped in. There was no coal in the bin but anchored to the back wall was a steel ladder leading up to a square steel door about two feet across. It was obviously the chute where coal was dumped into the bin and was bound to open to the outside of the building. I climbed the ladder and tugged on the lever which operated the locking mechanism. With a considerable amount of scraping and grinding, the rusty lever moved and the door creaked open. I silently thanked the architect who designed the coal chute into the basement.

I took a deep breath of the fresh moist air and climbed through the opening. I felt around in the darkness and my hand ran over a large tire of some sort. I pulled the steel door shut behind me and carefully stood up. As my eyes became accustomed to the shadowy darkness, I could see that the tire was part of a huge road grader parked next to the building. There was also a couple dump trucks, a cement mixer and several other pieces of heavy equipment around me. I took a few steps, tripped and fell face forward onto a pile of gravel. Obviously, the county used the area behind the courthouse to store road construction materials and equipment.

I looked up and saw that the windows of the entire third floor of the courthouse were ablaze with lights and I could hear loud voices coming from that direction. More cars could be heard arriving at the front of the building. From the sounds of all the commotion, everyone seemed to be far more interested in the capture of the murderer than my escape. Perhaps in all the uproar, the sheriff had taken the prisoner directly to the main jail on top floor and hadn't even discovered that I was missing.

Staying in the shadows of the road construction equipment, I worked my way toward the water tower at the back of the lot. When I reached the tower, I found that route of escape blocked by a six-foot chain link fence, topped with angle arms supporting three strands of barbed wire. They were angled to the outside to prevent anyone from climbing over the fence to get inside. They would also be nearly as effective in keeping anyone from climbing over from the inside to get out. I felt my way along the fence until I came to a large gate which was secured with a chain and a lock. I had escaped from the jail cell and then from the building, only to find myself still locked inside this yard.

I retraced my steps along the fence to the water tower. A steel ladder ran up one of the legs but it offered no escape route because it was set a good ten feet back from the fence. I continued along the fence to where it ended against the building. Almost as if someone had anticipated my need to escape from the yard, none of the heavy equipment had been parked close enough to allow it to used to scale the fence.

If there was no easy way to get out of this yard, then I would resort to force; I'd use one of the dump trucks to crash through the gate. I climbed into the cab of one of the trucks and felt around for the keys, but they were missing. The same was true for the other one. I was considering the possibility of getting the diesel engine started on the road grader when I noticed a stack of pierced steel planking of the type which had been used during the war to build emergency landing strips. We had put down miles of the same stuff building emergency strips in Korea. Each panel was about eighteen inches wide and ten feet long. There was a row of hooks along one edge and matching slots on the other to allow the panels to be locked together to form a stable landing surface. Three rows of round holes had been punched into each panel to give better traction for the airplanes.

By leaning one of the steel panels against the fence, I would be able to climb to the top where I could drop to the ground on the outside. I grabbed the end of the top panel on the stack and lifted, but it was a lot heavier than I had remembered. It took all of my strength to drag the panel to the fence and hoist one end up onto the angled barbed wire.

By sticking the toes of my shoes into the holes, I was able to use it like a ladder and climb right to the top. The only problem once that I got there was that the ground was some seven feet below me. Even when I was sixteen years old, a seven foot drop to hard ground would have been something to consider, but now that I was nearing sixty, I might as well have been taking a leap from the top of the courthouse.

I was standing at the top of the plank, balancing myself against the side of the courthouse when the decision was made for me. I heard a something which sounded like an air raid siren atop the court house. It began as a deep moan and then slowly increased in both volume and pitch until its wail could be heard for several miles. Evidently the sheriff had discovered that I was missing and had turned the thing on to signal the whole town of my escape. I tossed my backpack to the ground, sat down on the end of the plank, closed my eyes and dropped into the darkness.

CHAPTER TEN

The time that it took for me to drop the seven feet from the top of the chain link fence seemed like a lifetime. I hit the ground with a resounding thud. Searing pain shot up my right leg and converged in my lower back. I slammed back against the chain link fence and crumpled into a heap. I wished that I had learned how to do what skydivers euphemistically call a PLF, or a parachute landing fall. Properly executed, when a person hits the ground he allows his knees to bend and rolls to one side so his whole body absorbs the landing shock instead of concentrating it on his spine. My landing had more like a crunching flop.

I lay on the ground, perspiration beading up on my face and gasping for the breath which had been knocked out of me in the fall. My right ankle felt as if it had been crushed and searing pain radiated up and down my spine. All sorts of terrifying thoughts about broken bones, full body casts, traction devices and operations flooded through my mind.

When I had regained the ability to breathe, I gingerly flexed my ankle to see if it was going to bend in the proper directions or simply shoot forth more pain. Although my ankle felt as though it was badly sprained, it responded in the proper directions when asked. I decided to see if I could stand so I grabbed the fence, hoisted myself erect and placed some weight on my right leg. I took a few tentative steps while hanging onto the fence and when everything seemed to be working properly. At least, it appeared that I hadn't broken anything in the fall. There was still a considerable amount of pain in both my spine and ankle but I was able to walk. Urged on by the need to distance myself from there as quickly as possible and knowing that the main street was out of the question, I picked up my backpack and began to hobble slowly toward the dark street behind the courthouse. The residential area without street lights would offer me far more hiding places than would the business district.

In my concern that I might have broken something in the fall, I had blotted out the infernal howling of that siren on top of the courthouse. I heard the roar of an approaching car and dove for the cover of a small bush as it made a screeching turn onto the street where I was walking. Its headlights flashed across my hiding place as it roared past without stopping. I could hear other cars converging on the court house from various directions. Obviously the siren was used to summons all sorts of people in the event of a fire, air raid or natural disaster. I assumed that this time was for an escaped prisoner; me. From all of the activity which was being generated by the screaming of the siren, I was bound to be discovered if I didn't get out of sight in a hurry.

I reached the street behind the courthouse where the intersection was lighted by a dirty street lamp, ducked through the circle of yellow light and turned to the left in the direction of the airport. If I could make it to the Cub, I would hide there and take off at the slightest hint of dawn. At least I would have some mobility and a way to put distance behind me very rapidly. If it became necessary, I could manage a take off in the dark. Once in the air, I would have at least four hours of fuel and it didn't get light soon enough to see to land, I could always find an airport with a lighted runway by looking for its rotating beacon. I couldn't tell how high the clouds were, but it had stopped raining long ago and the visibility appeared to be a lot better.

The street was nearly pitch dark as the only light on it came from a few windows. There was no sidewalk along the street and I stumbled directly into a tree in the darkness. I decided that even though there were occasional cars coming and going, I could make much better time if I walked in the middle of the street. Each time that I heard one approaching, I would dart out of sight between houses or behind a bush.

I was about half way along the second block from the courthouse when I heard a car approaching so I stepped between a hedge and the porch of a dark house to let it pass. After it had gone by, a woman's voice behind me said, "We're going to have to stop meeting like this."

I froze in my tracks and turned my head in the direction from which the voice had come. I could see the red glow of a cigarette in the darkness. "Meeting like how?" I asked.

"I'm Maggie Nester, the waitress from the cafe," she replied. "It seems that every time that we meet, you are either already in trouble or getting into more of it."

"You gave me quiet a start. I didn't know you were there."

"I just took a bath and have been sitting out here on the porch, enjoying the cool air. I've been watching you ever since you left the courthouse."

"I certainly am in trouble, but whether you believe it or not, I haven't done anything wrong and the whole thing is a big mistake," I replied.

"I take it that the siren blowing at the courthouse means that you broke out of jail again. I'd say that your escaping twice in one night sets some sort of a record. That siren is the way the sheriff calls in his special deputies. I'll bet that he's having a cat fit right now."

"I don't really care to find out what kind of fit he might be having, I just want to find a way to get out of this town without getting caught."

"Well, I can tell you one thing for sure," Maggie said. "If you keep walking around on the streets, you'll get caught for sure. Why don't you come inside for a glass of lemonade and wait for things to cool off."

"I'd appreciate that, but considering that you are the one who started all of my troubles in the first place, why are you offering to help me now?"

"Well, I feel sort of guilty about being responsible for you getting arrested. When I showed the boss those three quarters in the cash register, he demanded to know who gave them to me. I told him that it was a some stranger and he called the sheriff. It didn't take a Pinkerton man to figure out that you were the only stranger in town. I guess the other reason for being nice to you is because I'd like to see what it would be like to be in bed with a man who travels around in a flying saucer."

I picked up instantly on what she said about going to bed but decided that the best way to handle such a situation was to simply ignore it. In the first place, I am a happily married man and secondly, there is a time and place for romantic trysts and here and now certainly was neither. "For something which is suppose to be a top secret, the news about me seems to have gotten around town awfully fast," I replied.

"Lillie came by the cafe for coffee this afternoon and told me about the telephone call you made to Texas and that you tried to call some number she had never heard of. Then she told me all about the call Sheriff Nester made to the FBI in Omaha. Lillie listens in on every phone call and then tells everything that she hears. Everybody in town knows better than to place a call when she is on duty if they don't want it repeated."

"You said that the sheriff's last name is Nester. That's the same as yours, are you related?"

"You might say that we were sort of related at one time. We were married for nearly twelve years, or at least we more or less married because we lived in the same house. He thought that making love was just like using his gun; pull it out, point and shoot. I finally realized that if he was in love with anything, it was his badge and gun."

My mouth was cotton dry and her offer of some lemonade was sounding better all the time. "I'll take you up on something to drink, if it's not too much trouble," I said.

She stubbed out her cigarette, took me by the hand and led me into the living room of her house. "You are limping pretty bad, are you hurt?" she asked.

I sprained an ankle when I jumped over the fence around the back of the courthouse, but I don't think that anything is broken," I answered.

She guided me through the darkness to a couch and said, "Have a seat and I'll get you a glass."

I slipped off my backpack and sat down on the couch. It was one of those soft, overstuffed things with lots of little loose pillows scattered around on it. I moved a couple of them out of my way and sank into its softness. I ran my hand over the fabric cover and it had a slick feeling, something like satin. I wondered what color it was.

From where I was sitting, I could see into the kitchen. She opened the refrigerator door and the light from it outlined her. She had a towel wrapped around her hair and was wearing a short robe which showed the greater part of her long legs. The view of her from the back in that short robe was far more interesting than had been the one of her in a starched waitress uniform.

I ran my hand over my ankle and could feel that it was hot and was swollen inside of my sock. "I don't suppose that you would have some ice for my ankle," I asked. "I seem to have sprained it pretty badly when I jumped over the fence."

"Sure thing," she replied as she rummaged around in a cabinet drawer and came up with one of those pleated rubber things with a screw lid. She took two aluminum ice trays out of the little freezing compartment in the refrigerator, ran water over them in the sink and twisted the ice cubes out. She put half of the cubes into the ice bag, dropped the rest into two glasses and filled them with liquid from a pitcher. When she replaced the pitcher and closed the door of the refrigerator, it was pitch dark again.

I could hear the ice clinking in the glasses and her bare feet scuffing lightly on the floor as she returned to the living room in the darkness. "Here you are," she said.

I reached out but instead of finding a cold glass, I found my hand touching one of her warm, smooth legs. She didn't move but I instinctively jerked away. When I felt the cold glass touch my arm, I fumbled to get hold of it before my groping hand found itself in places where it had no business being. She moved some of the throw pillows out of the way and sat down next to me. "Put your feet up here in my lap," she said.

I lifted my injured foot and turned to where it would be in her lap. She moved closer so my leg would lie across her lap with my foot resting on a pillow, then she reached down and lifted my other leg across her lap. I felt her loosen my shoe laces, removed my shoes and begin to rub the ice bag over my swollen ankle. "Your ankle is the size of a football," she said. "It's a wonder you can even walk."

She was sitting so close that I could feel the warmth of her body and the smoothness of the satin robe which she was wearing. It felt very much like the material which covered the couch. She wore no perfume but had a clean aroma of soap. She also smelled of cigarettes.

As we sipped the cold lemonade, I felt that I should say something, so I asked, "Do you know what time is it?"

I looked at the clock when I got the lemonade and it was a few minutes past ten," she replied.

She moved her warm hand slowly upward along my leg and my urge to respond to her touch was very compelling, but I resolved to be strong. I slid my hand under hers, picked it up and kissed her fingers. "Maggie, you are a beautiful and sexy lady, and your attention does great things for my ego, but I am a married man. Your suggestion is very tempting, and I'm truly sorry that this can go no further. I appreciate everything that you have done for me, but I feel that it would be best if I left now."

"Your wife is certainly a lucky woman," she said as she leaned over and kissed me lightly on the cheek. "I really got a rush the instant I laid eyes on you. It's too bad that all the good ones like you are always taken.

"Thanks for the very nice compliment, but I really should go," I told her as I fumbled in the darkness for my shoes.

"I can't stop you from leaving, but you won't last ten minutes if you walk out that door now."

"You'd call the sheriff?"

"Hell no. There's no love lost between him and me, but have you noticed all of those cars driving up and down the street. Every one of them has two or three men with guns in it and they are all searching for you. They aren't out there to arrest you; they are looking for target practice."

"What do you mean target practice?" I asked as a cold wave of fear swept over me.

"People have escaped from jail before but every one of them is pushing up daises now. According to the sheriff, they were all killed while resisting arrest when they were caught. I know how the sheriff and his special deputies work."

"Do you mean to tell me that the sheriff actually sends people out with the intention of killing someone instead of bringing them back alive?"

"That's exactly what I'm saying. You are just plain lucky that he didn't shoot you the first time you tried to escape. It wouldn't surprise me that he didn't tell Melvin to let you out."

"It's hard for me to believe such a situation exists. This sounds like a story about a crooked sheriff in some wild west town before the turn of the century, not 1946 in Nebraska." I said.

"You'd better believe it. Sheriff Nester runs this town with an iron fist," she replied. "There have been questions about whether some of the prisoners escaped from jail or were allowed to get out so that they could hunt them down and shoot them, but nothing was ever proven."

"That is a frightening thought."

"As I said, you will be better off here with me than out on the street. They would never think of looking for you here, so why don't you just sit here and rub your ankle with the ice bag while I dry my hair."

She closed the front door, lowered the shades on the living room windows and walked into the bedroom where she turned on a small radio on the bedside table. The soft music was the big band sound of Tommy Dorsey. She turned on a small bedside lamp and the light from it spilled out into the living room, giving me enough light to be able to see a little better. The room was neatly furnished with the couch, a couple chairs and a coffee table. Just as I suspected, the couch and chair were upholstered in a fabric with huge flowers on it. A large case filled with books ran along one wall and several framed photos hung on another.

Clamped to the back of a chair was of those strange looking hair dryers with a thing that looked like a big pot on it. She sat down, pulled the pot down over her head and turned it on. Since I had nothing else to do, I limped over to look at the photos on the wall. There weren't any of the usual family photos that one would expect to see, just several of a very beautiful young woman. She was dressed in short dresses and hats typical of the 1930s and was posed beside new automobiles and an airplane. There was also three framed magazine covers with her photo on them. I finally realized that the lady in the bedroom was the one in those photos.

I heard the hair dryer stop so I turned to return to the couch. From where I was standing, I could see into her bedroom. She had removed her robe and was combing her hair in front of a dresser with a large mirror. All that she was wearing was some thin baby-doll pajamas which left absolutely nothing to the imagination. In the image of her in the mirror, I could see her round breasts and erect nipples. She must be somewhere around forty years old, but she still had the body of a girl of twenty.

"Like what you see?" she asked with a smile.

Her question came as a shock because until then, I hadn't realized that by looking into the mirror, she could see me watching her from the living room. "I'm sorry, I didn't mean to stare."

"Don't apologize," she said as she turned sideways, thrust out her breasts and struck a provocative pose. "I'm proud of my figure and work hard to keep it looking good. At one time, it made me a lot of money as a photographer's model."

"I surmised that you were a model from all those photos over there on the wall. I also see that you made some magazine covers, I'm impressed."

"Not only did I pose for photographers, but I was also in a couple movies."

"I don't mean to be personal, but why did you leave a successful movie and modeling career and how in the world did you end up married to a redneck sheriff in a dinky little town in Nebraska?" I asked as I leaned against the frame of the bedroom door.

"Both of those questions have the same answer. I came out here for an advertising photo session for a new line of farm equipment. I was twenty-two at the time and thought that I had a firm control over my emotions, but when I met a handsome sheriff, I fell head over heels in love. The rest is history."

"The sheriff said something about his son being killed in the war. Considering that he must have been eighteen or older at the time, I take it that he wasn't your son."

"No, he was from a former marriage. He was twelve when we got married. In fact, I found out later that the sheriff had been married twice before he married me.

Maggie removed the bedspread, folded it neatly and placed it on a chest at the foot of the bed. The bed had a fancy iron frame with cast joints and finals. In 1986, a wrought iron bed like that would bring close to a thousand dollars in an antique store. She turned back the sheets, pointed to the bed and said, "Are you going to join me or just stand there admiring the scenery?"

This was by far the best offer that I'd had since I arrived at this place and, what the heck, I might never get back to 1986 and who could ask for a better way to be trapped. I hung my jacket over the foot of the bed and began to unbutton my shirt.

CHAPTER ELEVEN

We lay there in the darkness, basking in the after-glow of lovemaking. She picked up a pack of Luckies, shook out a couple and offered one to me.

"No thanks," I said. "I don't smoke."

She struck a kitchen match, waited for the sulphur to burn away, held the flame to the tip of the cigarette and took a deep draw. She held it for a few seconds and blew it toward the ceiling. "Did you really come here in a flying saucer?" she asked.

"Not exactly. I did come here by air, but not in a flying saucer or space ship."

"Where did you really come from? Is your home here on earth or did you come from Mars or some place like that?" she asked.

"As dull as it might sound, I am totally human and I live right here on earth, in Colorado."

"Melvin said that you came in a flying saucer and got left here when he almost caught it. He said that people will be coming to rescue you with ray guns."

"Melvin has a rather vivid imagination. It's true that I come from a place a considerable distance from here, not so much in distance as in time. I seem to have moved backwards forty years through some sort of time warp to get here. When I left home this morning, the year was 1986."

"What's a time warp?" she asked.

"It's a rather complicated theory that if a person can travel at the speed of light, he can move either forward or backward through time."

"How fast did you have to go to get here?" she asked.

"Actually, only about sixty miles an hour, but evidently something that I don't understand happened along the way."

"How are you going to get back to where you belong, or are you trapped here forever?" she asked.

"I wish that I knew those answers myself. Since I don't know how I got here, I have no idea how to go about getting out of this situation. One thing for sure, I can't sit still until the sheriff finds me again so I am going to have to do something. No telling what he might do if he gets hold of me again."

"That's certainly true. The sheriff is a vicious, sadistic man who gets pleasure from hurting people. That's the reason why we aren't married any longer."

I wanted to ask her more about that subject but decided that I would be digging into a personal area where I had no business. Perhaps it was also a subject about which I didn't really want to know.

She stubbed out the cigarette in an ashtray on the bedside table, laid her head on my shoulder and became very quiet. I guessed that she was trying to fathom what I had told her. She was probably also wondering whether I telling the truth or was simply some sort of nut. Either way, she didn't seem to be in a hurry to kick me out into the street or turn me back over to the law.

The street in front of her house was gravel and I could hear the crunching of tires as cars drove past. Most of them seemed to be going very slowly and occasionally, I could see the flash of a spotlight as it swept across the house. Obviously, they were still looking for me.

I guessed the time to be around midnight and it had been more than an hour since I heard the last car drive past. Maggie's steady breathing told me that she had dozed off. She was probably tired from a long day on her feet and a good romp in bed was all that she needed to put her to sleep. I felt that it was now safe enough for me to try to get to the airport so I tried to pull my arm from beneath her neck. She stretched, yawned and snuggled close to me. Her hair smelled clean.

"Are you awake?" she whispered

"Maggie, I think that it's time for me to go. I hate to ask any more favors of you, but do you have a car?"

"No, I don't have one. I got this house in the divorce settlement, but we never owned a car. He always had the sheriff's car to drive so he never needed to buy one," she replied. "I suppose that I'm lucky to have gotten the house because neither of his other wives got diddly-squat when they left him. You met one of them, Lillie, the telephone operator. She was his first wife and the mother of the son who was killed in the war."

"In small towns like this, it seems that everyone is related to one another in some manner and everyone knows what is going on. I'll bet that people have to be careful what they say or do around here."

"That's certainly true. It wouldn't surprise me a bit if everyone in town didn't already know that you and I were in bed together tonight," she said with a laugh.

"And here I thought that we were being so discreet."

"Are you sure that you have to go?" she asked as she snuggled her warm body closer to mine and ran her fingers up my neck and into my hair.

"As tempting as I find your offer, I'm afraid that I do have to go," I told her as I disengaged her arms from around my neck.

"If you need for me to take you somewhere, I could borrow a car. My boss has one and I'm sure that he would loan it to me."

"That's OK, it's not that far to where I need to go. I'll just walk there."

"Where do you need to go?" she asked.

"Maggie, considering what you have told me about the sheriff, it's really better that you don't know."

"Why, don't you trust me?"

"It's not you, it's the sheriff that I don't trust. There's no telling what he might do if he thought you had helped me escape."

She turned on the small bedside lamp and slipped on her robe. When I had dressed and picked up my backpack, she turned off the light, took my hand and walked to the front door with me. She stepped onto the porch, looked both ways to be sure that the street was clear and said, "I'm afraid for you and hate to see you go."

"I'll be fine and thanks again for all that you have done for me."

"No matter what it takes, don't let the sheriff and his men catch you. They have killed people before and will probably do so again," she whispered with a little sniff as she clung tightly to my hand.

"If I can make to daylight, I'll be long gone from here," I told her.

She put her arms around my neck and pressed her warm body against me. I could feel tears on her cheeks. "Please be careful and take care of yourself," she whispered as she gave me a lingering, wet kiss.

CHAPTER TWELVE

I stepped off the porch, limped out into the street and stopped to listen. The town was as quiet as a tomb. While my ankle still hurt and had become stiff but at least I could walk on it without getting a sharp shot of pain with each step. The night seemed to have changed as there was a lot less moisture in the air, the wind had stopped blowing and it even seemed to be a bit warmer. I looked up to see if I could see any stars. but it was still overcast. There seemed to be a bit more light in the sky than when I escaped because I could now make out the shape of houses and trees along the street. I heard the lock on Maggie's door click behind me.

I walked along the middle of the street to the end of the block, stopped to listen again and crossed the intersection. I could see the dark bulk of two cars parked in front of a house. I ran my hand along the side of the first one until I felt the door handle. I tried to turn it but it was locked. I moved to the next car, turned the handle and the door opened with a rusty creak. I felt around on the dash for the ignition switch but could not find it. Just as I was about to give up, I realized that it was an old model Ford with the ignition key on the side of the steering column. There was a key in the switch and it turned easily. I slid into the driver's seat, pushed the switch lever forward, depressed the clutch pedal and felt around on the dash for the starter button. I pressed it but nothing happened. Evidently, the battery was either dead or missing. There was no hope here so I stepped out, turned the handle and closed the door to the first notch to keep from making any noise.

In the next block, I came to a pickup truck and as I reached to open the door, I heard a chain rattle beside the house and the deep growl of a dog. I froze in my tracks and waited. If he came after me, I could probably avoid him by climbing on top of the cab but then he would have me trapped. Once a dog has something up a tree, so to speak, they will stay with it for hours. The dog growled again and began to bark. From inside the house a gruff voice shouted, "Shaddup, you damn mutt."

The dog stopped barking but continued to growl softly. I knew that if I opened the door on the pickup or did anything else, it would set him to barking again. With the dog's owner already awake, the best thing to do was slip quietly away. I figured that it was time for me to give up trying to become a car thief and limped on toward the east edge of town. My ankle still hurt but it did seem to be getting better with a little use.

When I could no longer see houses on either side of the street, I had to pick my way carefully as I didn't want to tumble into a ditch or something worse. The surface beneath my feet changed from gravel to grass and I knew that I had not only reached the end of town, but also the end of that street. I would have to turn one way or the other and the only direction which I knew would take me to the airport also led back to the main street. I hadn't heard anything or seen any cars since leaving Maggie's place, but in light of what she had said about the sheriff and his special deputies, I was sure that they hadn't given up looking for me. Perhaps they were going to wait until daylight to renew their search.

Just as I turned to my left toward the main street, I heard a new sound coming from the direction of the courthouse. It sounded like dogs. The frightening thing was that those dogs weren't barking, they were baying in the same way that bloodhounds do when they are hot on the scent of an animal. These people were really serious about finding me if they had gone to the trouble of bringing out the dogs to track me down. I wondered how the dogs had picked up my scent, but then I remembered having dropped my handkerchief on the bed in the jail. What better than a sweaty handkerchief to give the dogs a good scent to work from.

This situation was really getting serious, I had to get some distance between me and those dogs and had to do it in a hurry. I started out down the street, half walking and half trotting. I hadn't gone more than a block when a dog came charging out from behind a house, barking and raising a real ruckus. I could tell from his bark that he wasn't a very large dog and could probably do me no real harm, but if he kept it up very long, he was bound to attract attention. I decided that the best thing to do was to continue walking as fast as possible and he would probably stop barking once I had left his territory.

I was wrong. That mangy little mutt kept right at my heels, barking and yapping away for two blocks until I got to the Studebaker place. If I didn't get rid of that little noise maker, the men with the bloodhounds would probably hear him and come directly there after me. There was a single bare bulb burning above the door to the shop. It was dim and coated with dirt but it furnished enough illumination for me to find a rock. It was a lucky throw as the rock whapped the little mutt in the side and he went yelping for home. There were two cars parked outside of the building and I checked each one for keys. Neither of them was locked, but there was no keys in them either. I considered the possibility of trying to hot wire one of them but decided that it would take too much time and since it was parked outside of a garage, it probably wouldn't run anyway.

134

I tried to remember all of the old movies that I had seen in which escaped prisoners were running from bloodhounds and how they threw them off their trail. Most of the things that I could remember were either too ridiculous to work or else didn't and the gangsters were captured in the end. I thought about the old trick of wading in a creek, but there certainly wasn't any water around. Then I remembered where an escaped prisoner took some ammonia with him and sprinkled it on the ground as he ran. When the dogs got a snootful of the ammonia, they couldn't smell anything and he got away. The only problem was the fact that I had no ammonia and there was little chance of my finding any.

I could hear the dogs baying, but they were still a long way off. It was difficult to tell just where they were because it seemed that every other dog in town had added their voices to the night. Since I had already walked around and left my scent at the Studebaker place, I might as well try to confuse them as much as possible. I walked all the way around the building, stopping at each door and rubbing my hand on the knob. There was a ladder leaning against the back of the building so I scuffed my feet around it and rubbed my hands over the rungs. The more places they had to search, the more time I would have to escape.

Just as I was about to leave, I noticed a bucket of old engine oil beside the garage door. It wasn't ammonia, but might just do the trick and kill my scent enough to make then lose the trail. I picked up the bucket and retraced my steps about a hundred feet back up the street in the direction from which I came. Then I took three or four very long steps to the opposite side of the road,

135

pouring oil on each spot where I had put my foot down. Perhaps the dogs would miss where I left the trail and would have to spend a lot of time sniffing around the building. I was buying time and time was what I needed.

I tossed the empty bucket as far away as I could, turned east on the paved road toward the airport and began walking as rapidly as my sprained ankle would allow. I knew better than to try to run, even if I could have. Running would tire only me out, making it easy for the dogs to overtake me. Even with a sprained ankle, I knew that I could walk much further than I could ever run or jog.

I paused for a second to catch my breath and listen to the dogs which were still well behind me. Suddenly, they stopped baying and began to bark with excitement, the way that dogs do when they run something up a tree. Then it struck me, they had probably followed my trail to Maggie's house and thinking that I was inside, were barking at her door. The sheriff was bound to know that I had been there and that she had helped me. Considering what she had said about how vicious he is, there was no telling what he might do to her. After all, in light of the fact that she got the house when she divorced him, she was probably not one of his favorite people. I wondered if he would actually arrest her for helping me escape. She had been so nice to me and I sincerely hoped that she wouldn't get into trouble.

I saw the headlights of a car turn into the street at the west end of town and head in my direction, so I began to search for a place to hide. There were no houses or bridges around and the only cover that I could find was some weeds in the ditch beside the road. They weren't more than a foot high, but by lying still in them, a person driving by at night might not notice. I pulled off my backpack in order to get as low as possible and flattened myself in the weeds. I lay there for quite a while but the car never passed. When I finally raised my head for a look, there was nothing in sight. I had lost a lot of time that I could have used to put distance between me and the dogs. I had also learned a lesson. The next time that I had to hide, I would lie down facing toward the oncoming car so I could see if it turned off or not.

I could hear that the dogs baying again, indicating that they had left Maggie's place and were back on my trail. From the location of their sound, I estimated that they would soon reach the street which led to the Studebaker place. I had only about a quarter mile lead on them.

I had taken only a few steps when the odor of cigarette smoke wafted by. I froze in my tracks because as strong as it was, it couldn't have come from very far away. I strained my eyes and ears and then I saw a red glow become brighter as someone took another puff. Then I made out the dark shape of a car parked on the shoulder of the road no more than twenty yards away ahead of me. The sheriff must have set up a roadblock on all the roads leading out of town and I had almost stumbled into one of them in the dark. As I watched, another glow appeared beside the first one; there must be at least two people there.

Then I heard someone in the car say, "I think that sitting out here in the middle of the road is nothing but a wild goose chase. Melvin said that people in a flying saucer would pick him up and I'll bet that he is already long gone."

"That certainly wasn't a wild goose that you were chasing me with a few minutes ago," came a woman's voice with a laugh.

"It may not have been a goose, but you'll have to admit that it was plenty wild. I'll bet that your old man would have a fit if he knew that you were getting a little while he was out of town."

"He'd have a fit if he thought that I was getting a little anywhere; you know how some husbands are about things like that. Turn on the switch so we can play the radio," she said. A few seconds later, I heard music.

It was easy to see why they hadn't heard me approaching; they were occupied in other ways, but I still had to pass by them some way. The railroad ran parallel to the highway and I didn't remember seeing a fence between them as I had walked to town. Feeling my way in the darkness with each step, I moved carefully off the road toward the tracks.

The baying of the dogs was now much louder and I looked back toward town. I could see the lights of several vehicles on the road leading toward the Studebaker place. I could clearly make out two men with dogs on leashes in the beams of their headlights. At the rate that they were traveling and with the roadblock ahead, it wouldn't be very long before they would catch up with me. I had to do something and do it mighty fast.

138

I worked my way down into a ditch and up the other side, then I felt crushed rock under my feet. Two steps later, my foot struck a rail. I stepped between the rails and began to walk as fast as possible in the dark. I looked back and could see that the men and dogs had reached the Studebaker place and were searching around it for me. All sorts of possibilities ran through my mind. Perhaps I had been able to throw them off my trail with the motor oil or else they would think that I had stolen a car and gotten away.

It is hard enough to walk on cross ties in the daylight, but doing it in the dark without tripping is really difficult, but I kept moving as fast as I could. I had traveled what I estimated to be a hundred yards when I heard the car which had been blocking the road start its engine and saw the headlights come on. It drove up to where the other cars were parked around the Studebaker place. Since the people blocking the road had returned and the dogs hadn't picked up my trail again, they might decide that I had escaped for good and give up. I crossed the ditch back to the road where it would be easier walking.

I continued on toward the airport, stopping every minute or so to look back and listen to see if the dogs sounded as if they were on my trail again. They seemed to still be involved around the Studebaker place and perhaps all of those people milling around would cover my trail to the point that the dogs would never be able to pick it up again.

I was now getting well ahead of the dogs and almost to the airport when I saw a dark bulk off to the right of the road. I realized that it was the abandoned farm house that I had seen as I had walked to town. It was only a short distance from the airport and would be a good place for me to hide and rest until it was light enough to see. It was still so dark that it was impossible to see the horizon and if I attempted to take off now, I might either climb into the clouds or else fly right into the ground. There certainly wasn't any lights or instruments on the airplane to help me.

I felt my way along until I came to the porch, then through the open door. It was pitch dark inside the house so I felt around in my back pack for shaving kit where I kept a small flashlight. While I was at it, I checked the time on the travel alarm clock and dropped it into my pocket. It was a little past three, another hour and a half or two before it would be light enough to see.

I covered the lens on the flashlight with my fingers to let out just enough light to allow me to see what was in the place. Other than an old couch against one wall, the living room was empty. There was an ancient wood-burning stove in the kitchen, along with a pile of trash in one corner. The other two rooms on the lower floor contained nothing except some old clothing scattered about.

A flight of stairs led from the living room to the floor above where two bedrooms were located. There was a row of low trees between the house and town so I climbed to the second floor where I would have a better view of what my pursuers were doing. There was an old bed with open springs and a cotton mattress in one of the bedrooms, along with several empty beer bottles. I also noted several used condoms scattered about on the floor. Evidently, this old house was a favored place for teenagers to indulge themselves. In the other room was a chair with a broken back and an old dresser without any drawers.

From the window on the west side, I could see the lights of cars around the Studebaker place and an occasional flick of a flashlight indicated that someone was on the roof. Perhaps they had bought my trick and thought that I had somehow gotten inside the building. I wished that I had taken Melvin's pistol when I left the jail. If I had, they would know that I was armed and would have to be far more careful when searching for me. If they were forced to be careful during their search, it would have given me more time. I sat down on the window sill where I could keep an eye on what was going on in town and wait for daylight to arrive.

CHAPTER THIRTEEN

It seemed as if the time would never pass. I would wait for what I would estimate to be at least half an hour and then flick on the flashlight for a second to look at the clock. Usually, no more than five minutes would have passed since the last time that I had checked.

It was around half past three when the activity around the Studebaker place ceased and I began to hear the dogs baying again. I could also see the glare of headlights coming along the road toward the airport. It was obvious that the ploy of

142

sprinkling motor oil on my tracks to throw the dogs off hadn't worked and they had their noses on my trail again.

I knew that in order to hold my scent, the dogs would have to follow my trail from the road to the railroad tracks where I went around the roadblock and then back again, all of which would give me more time to plan my strategy. They had proven one thing for certain, those dogs could hang onto my trail no matter what I did to throw them off. I knew that in due time, they would lead the sheriff right to this house. Since it was now a race between their catching up with me and the arrival of enough daylight to see to fly, I needed to buy all of the time that I possibly could.

The first thing to do was to make it necessary for the sheriff to have to search every inch of this house before they could go any further. Above the landing of the stairs was a framed opening leading into the attic, so I would make it appear that I was hiding there. I dragged the dresser to a spot beneath the opening and put the chair on top of it. Perhaps this would make them think that I had used it to climb into the attic. I rubbed my hands over the dresser and chair in order to leave as much of my scent as possible.

In the closet of one of the downstairs rooms was a trap door which opened into the crawl space beneath the house. I used my pocket knife to pry it open, urinated onto the dirt below it and closed it. The dogs were sure to be attracted to that place also. Now, they would have to search both places before they could leave the house. Judging by the amount of time that they had spent looking for me at the Studebaker place, searching the attic and under floor should take the better part of an hour and bring daylight a lot closer.

I went back upstairs to check on the progress of the men and dogs. From my vantage point, I could see that they had trailed me to where I left the road and crossed the ditch to the railroad tracks. They weren't making very good time and I would still have time to create more diversions to keep them busy.

From what I remembered about the barn behind the house, it was a huge thing with a hay loft and several doors and windows. I stepped out the back door of the house and, shielding the flashlight so that only a thin slit of light fell on the ground, walked directly to the barn.

This particular barn was typical of most such structures found in the Midwest, with a wide aisle through the middle so wagons or trucks could be driven in one end and out the other. Large doors closed the ends of the drive-through for weather protection. The doors at the back end of the barn were closed but one of the front doors had come off its hinges and was laying on the ground. There were stalls and feed rooms along either side of the aisle and near both the front and rear of the barn were ladders leading to the hay loft above. The musty smell of straw and cow manure still hung in the air, along with the aroma of skunks. Smelling skunks around deserted barns is not all that unusual because they are a natural haven for mice which attracts them. The natural aroma of a skunk is so strong that it doesn't have to spray

144

in order for the telltale smell to linger for hours or days after it has gone.

It would be useless for me to try to delay the sheriff by going into each stall or feed room because it would take him only a few seconds to let the dogs check them out. Searching the loft would be another matter because the dogs couldn't get up there and it would have to be done by a person. I climbed the ladder closest to the door to find that the loft was stacked high with bales of fresh hay. Even though the farm was deserted, evidently the owner still used the barn to store hay. I had to scramble over the top of the stacks of bales in order to reach the ladder at the other end of the barn. Without the dogs to help sniff me out, doing a complete search of the hay bales in the loft might occupy them long enough for me to escape by air.

I climbed down the ladder at the back end of the barn and tried to open the large doors. Evidently, they had not been used in many years and dirt had blown against them, making them impossible to open. I figured that there must be another way out of the back of the barn so I began checking the individual stalls. As I stepped into the second one from the end, I saw the outline of something moving near the opposite wall and I the skunk smell was much stronger. I froze in my tracks and aimed my flashlight toward the movement. A mother skunk with five little ones scampered around in the beam of light, appearing not to be the slightest bit frightened. About the only real enemy that the skunk has is the great horned owl and I suppose that she realized that owls don't carry flashlights.

Skunks seldom spray unless they are threatened, but as a warning that I was invading her territory, she rushed a few steps toward me with her tail raised high, stopped and stamped her front feet on the floor. The young skunks seemed to be totally unconcerned about what was going on and continued to dig around in a pile of hay, searching for something edible. There was an open window on the opposite side of the stall which would be an ideal escape route if I could get past the mother skunk guarding her brood.

I moved as far away from the mother skunk as I could and worked my way along the side of the stall toward the window, constantly watching for any sign that she was about to become more defensive. She held her ground, waving her tail over her back and stamped her feet. I reached the window and climbed through. Skunks seem to be far more tolerant of humans than they are of dogs and if those bloodhounds follow my scent into that stall, they are in for the surprise of their lives. If they provoke that mother skunk and she gives them a shot of her spray, they probably won't be able to smell me or anything else for a month.

I walked about fifty yards from the barn before I came to a barbed wire fence which separated that property from the airport. A shelter belt of trees along the west side of the house blocked my view of the men coming along the road but I could tell from their sound that they were getting rather close. I had to move fast. As one last bit of diversion in the event that they got past the skunk, I walked along the fence back toward the road to a point where I could see the approaching cars. They were still far enough away that they couldn't spot me in the headlights, but they were getting much too close for comfort. I retraced my steps along the fence to a point near where I had first reached it, spread the strands of barbed wire and crawled through. Perhaps they would follow my scent along the fence and miss where I had crawled through. At least I was now on the airport and could see the dark outline of the hangars on the opposite side of the grass runway.

It was a hundred yards or more yards from the fence to the hangars and my first thought was to head directly to the hangar where the Cub was located but decided to give myself every advantage possible by leaving my trail of scent to the PT-19 which was tied down well to the south of the hangars. When I arrived at the ship, I walked around the left wingtip and along its trailing edge to the fuselage as if I was going to get into it. I climbed up on the wing, slid over the fuselage in front of the windshield and walked on top the right wing to the tip where I dropped to the ground. Even that short drop sent a stab of pain into my ankle.

It was about fifty yards from where the PT-19 was tied down to the hangar where I had put the Cub and if the dogs should follow my trail that far, there was no need for me to attempt to throw them off again. I hurried to the hangar and slid one of the doors open enough for me to slip inside. I turned the flashlight on for a second to be sure that the Cub was still there and ready to go. My note was still on the seat and everything appeared to be just like when I left it.

I would probably have to take off in a hurry as soon as it became light enough to see and I needed to get the Cub out ofthe hangar and into a position for a quick takeoff. Also, I wanted to get the doors of the hangar open before the sheriff and his men came close enough to hear them being moved. I could hear the dogs baying as they trailed me down the road and hoped that all the barking and baying would cover the noise that the doors were bound to make. There is no quiet way to open steel hangar doors, so I shoved them open as quickly as possible in order to reduce the amount of time that they would be making noise. The dogs evidently hadn't heard me open the doors because they were still had their noses to the ground and were going strong. I strapped my backpack under the front seatbelt, rolled the Cub outside and turned it to line up with the runway.

This was the first time that I could remember doing a preflight in total darkness but I did my best. It made no difference whether the oil might be low or not because I had none with me, so I didn't bother trying to check it. I felt of the wire sticking out of the front fuel tank cap and it indicated that the tank was full. I ran my hands over the wingtips, moved the ailerons and felt of the rear control surfaces. Movement of the stick felt normal and I could hear the cables and surfaces moving. Satisfied that everything was working as it should, I checked the magneto switches to be sure that they were off, turned the fuel selector to the front tank and pulled the prop through a few compressions to pull a charge of fuel into each cylinder. The little Continental had started on the first pull every time that I had cranked it before and I hoped that it would not fail me when I was going to need it the most. I turned the magneto switches on, cracked the throttle slightly for starting and went around on the opposite side of the ship where I wouldn't be visible from the house in case someone should shine a spotlight in that direction. I figured they were used to seeing airplanes outside and wouldn't think anything of it. I sat down on the left tire to wait.

CHAPTER FOURTEEN

I didn't have long to wait before headlight beams flashed across the airport as cars turned into the drive in front of the vacant house. I counted the number of times that headlights flashed across in order to know how many cars were arriving. They must have gathered more searchers because eleven cars turned into the drive. The dogs stopped baying and began to bark in the same manner that I had heard them do each time that they thought that they had me located.

The sheriff's gruff voice came through the darkness, "I know that you are in there, so come out with your hands up," he shouted.

I leaned forward so I could look under the fuselage to see what was going on. The house was bathed in the light from the headlights of the cars parked in a circle around it. Two or three of the cars had spotlights and were playing them on the upstairs windows. I could also see several people standing on the front porch, carrying shotguns and rifles. I could also see that most of the men were carrying bottles from which they took swigs now and then. Not only was I being chased by a bunch of men with itchy trigger fingers, they were also drunk. There seemed to be a lot of booze around for a state which was supposed to be dry. It wouldn't surprise me if the sheriff wasn't also the local bootlegger. Seems that they usually were.

"I'm giving you one last chance to surrender or we are going to send the dogs in after you," yelled the sheriff.

"What the hell, let's set the place on fire. That'll flush him out," shouted a man standing on the porch.

"Don't nobody strike no matches and don't nobody start shooting neither," yelled the sheriff. "You're liable to hit one of us."

I could hear the dogs barking as they searched through the house. Most of the activity seemed to be concentrated on the second floor and then I heard a loud crash. "You find him?" yelled the sheriff, who was still standing in the yard and playing the beam of his long flashlight across the upstairs windows.

"Naw, that was Clarence. He was up in the attic and fell through the damn ceiling. I think he broke his leg," came an answer from a man who poked his head out of an upstairs window.

There was a considerable amount of talking and yelling for the next several minutes as they carried a man out the front door and laid him in the back of a pickup. One of the people in the pickup yelled, "Wait till we get back before you flush him out. We want to be here for the fun." The engine of the pickup started and it roared off toward town.

The true impact of what Maggie had told me about the special deputies really came home when I heard that. Those men had every intention of killing me when they found me. I looked toward the east, hoping for any signs of approaching dawn. It was still dark but it did seem that the whole sky was turning slightly gray. I wasn't sure whether it was actually getting lighter or just the reflection of the car lights on the low overcast.

"He's under the floor," came a shout from inside the house and the activity shifted back to the lower floor. I could hear the muffled barking of the dogs as they searched for me beneath the house.

After the dogs had searched the crawl space and determined that I wasn't there, the sheriff called all of the men to the front of the house and told the men with the dogs, "He ain't in the house so he must have gone to the barn. Everybody stand back and let the dogs see if they can pick up his scent again."

The men who were holding the dogs held out something for the dogs to smell and they began to bay again. I guessed that it was the handkerchief that I had carelessly left in the jail that they were using to give them my scent. I certainly would have been more careful about leaving something like that behind if I had even guessed that they would bring out the dogs to search for me. So much for hindsight. While all of this was happening, three more cars arrived. With all the laughing and yelling, the place was beginning to take on the atmosphere of a county fair. The whole town must be awake and hunting for me.

It was almost surreal, sitting there watching armed, drunken men searching for me no more than the length of a football field away. The men with the dogs began to sweep back and forth across the area between the house and the barn and suddenly the dogs really let it out. They had picked up my trail again and were headed for the barn. Perhaps the diversions that I had left for them there would keep them busy long enough for me to be able to see to take off. Dark or not, I was determined to crank the engine and go for it the instant that the dogs lead them through the fence and onto the airport.

When the dogs stopped baying and began to bark, everyone converged on the barn. "He's in the hay loft," shouted one of the dog handlers from inside the barn.

"Three or four of you men go up there and find him," shouted the sheriff.

"Hell, let's just set fire to the place and smoke him out," shouted another.

"Like hell you will," came another voice. "This is my barn and I got hay stored in there."

153

Cars were backed up and turned around so their headlights would shine on the door of the barn and a couple of them drove to the opposite end. Spotlights came on and illuminated the hayloft doors. There was a lot shouting going on inside the barn as they searched for me.

The loft doors swung open and someone stuck their head out and shouted, "There's a million bales of hay up here and he could be hiding under any of them."

"I say that we burn him out," came a shout from the growing crowd in front of the barn.

"Set the place on fire," yelled another.

Mixed in with the confusion of noise of the hunt, the dogs were adding their voices to the fray. Suddenly they began to yelp and howl as all bedlam broke loose. Dogs and men came running and tumbling out the door of the barn, swearing and yelling. "Skunks! The place is full of skunks!" There was the sound of several shots being fired inside the barn as they killed the mother skunk and her babies.

Several of the men began to mill around the front of the barn and shout, "Burn the place! Set it on fire! Smoke him out!"

I flinched as I heard a shot. In an attempt to get the attention of the mob, the sheriff had fired his pistol into the air and was shouting, "Don't do it men. This barn belongs to Homer Watson."

"You burn my barn and you will all pay for it," shouted Homer.

154

It was too late to stop the drunken mob. Someone was already splashing gasoline around inside the barn and a few seconds later, the glow of fire could be seen through the doors and windows. Smoke began to roll out of the open loft doors.

"Get your guns ready and get him as he comes out," someone shouted.

The flames went after the dry hay in the barn like a tornado goes after a mobile home park. Within seconds after the fire was started, flames were licking out of windows and shooting from the hay loft doors. A large round area of the roof began to glow and suddenly it fell in, sending a spray sparks and flames into the air. The flames were lighting up everything as bright as day. The men began to fall back from the heat which was so intense that I could even feel it where I was.

I had been so absorbed in watching the men setting fire to the barn that I had neglected to watch for the approach of dawn. I looked to the east and could see the horizon against a dull gray sky. I had forgotten just how rapidly the change from total darkness to dawn comes in the late summer. It was time for me to make my move. I hoped that the men would be so engrossed in the burning barn that I could escape undetected. With the dog's noses full of skunk spray, they certainly wouldn't be able to trail me and perhaps the men would think that I had perished in the fire. Probably the smartest thing to have done was stayed out of sight and waited for them to finally leave, but the animal instinct of fear and flight took over my good judgment.

155

I stepped in front of the Cub and spun the prop. Nothing happened! I pulled it again and still no response. I knew that I had turned the magneto switches on after I primed it, but the engine refused to start. My throat was cotton dry as I pulled the prop again before finally realizing that the fuel charges that I had pulled into the cylinders an hour before had long since evaporated.

On these older engines, the throttle has to be completely closed in order for the idle mixture to be rich enough to prime the cylinders for starting. I reached inside the cockpit and closed the throttle but left the switches on so that it would start as soon as gas reached the spark plugs. A cold engine will start with a closed throttle but it usually won't run for more than a few seconds unless the throttle is cracked to give a faster idle.

As I stepped back in front of the ship to spin the prop again, I heard someone yelling, "There he is. He's got an airplane!"

"Get him. Don't let him escape," shouted some else.

I didn't dare to pause long enough to look at the person who had spotted me as I pulled the prop through. One pull, two pulls and finally the little engine caught on the third pull and began to cough and sputter. I lunged past the spinning prop and grabbed for the throttle to get it opened to a fast idle before the engine died.

Just as I reached inside the cockpit and nudged the throttle, I heard guns firing. One bullet kicked up dirt a few feet in front of the Cub and I heard another one slam into the metal of the hangar. One of the benefits, if you could call it that, of being shot at

156

by drunken people instead of sober ones is that they usually aren't very good shots. Using the old saw that they couldn't hit the side of a barn didn't fit here as I could hear more bullets slamming into the hangar. Then I heard one crash a window in the office behind me.

The usual way to enter the rear seat of a Cub is from behind the wing struts, but I wasn't about to waste the time that it would take to duck under the struts and get into the seat the normal way. I jerked the throttle about half way open and barked both shins as I struggling over the struts. The cold engine sputtered in protest as it began to pick up speed.

My unusual entry was far from graceful and the ship was already beginning to move forward when I was able to turn around and plop into the seat with my right leg still hanging out the door. I could hear more gunshots and felt a puff of wind as a bullet whizzed in front of my face and smashed through the sliding Plexiglas window. Had I have been in the front seat, it would have struck me in the head.

I shoved the throttle all the way forward but the cold engine refused to come up to full power. It coughed and sputtered along at about half power, far less than what would be required to get me off the ground. My only hope was that the I could pick up enough speed to get out of their range and that the engine would come up to takeoff power before I reached the end of the runway.

The Cub suddenly begin to veer to the right and I glanced out to see a man clinging to the right wingtip, dragging it back. He was hanging on with one hand and trying to find something to grab with the other one. I was going faster than he could run but he kept hanging on with one hand and sort of swinging and bouncing his feet against the ground. If he should ever get his feet in front of his body and dig his heels into the ground, he could easily bulldog the ship around in a ground loop.

I jammed full left rudder and stabbed the left brake with my heel. The ship responded by veering to the left, which whipped the wingtip free of his grip and sent him tumbling head over heels. The engine was beginning to pick up power and the tail came up as I gained speed, but was still too slow to get off the ground.

I looked to the right and could see a pickup with several men in the back racing along the other side of the fence which separated the airport from the farm. Fortunately for me, the men couldn't aim their guns and shoot because they were having to hang on in order to keep from being thrown out as the pickup bounded over the rough ground. Suddenly the driver swerved the pickup into the fence, ripped through it and began to race at an angle which would put him ahead of me when he reached the runway.

The engine was now hitting on all four cylinders and running smoothly now but for some reason I simply wasn't accelerating fast enough to get off the ground. I glanced at the tach which was indicating only 1800 rpm, a good 300 below what it should be turning. It was then that I finally realized that the carburetor heat was still on. I had forgotten to turn it off before starting the engine. Had I been able to do a normal pre-takeoff check, I would have found it but there was no time for such amenities. With the heat on, the engine would barely develop cruise power. One might be able to get off the ground with the carb heat on, but it would take a very long run. I fumbled for the knob and shoved it forward.

The little Continental surged up to full power just as the driver of the pickup swerved in front of me and slammed on his brakes. The men in the back tumble forward as the pickup skidded to a stop, then began to untangle themselves and grab for their guns. I was less than a hundred yards from the pickup but I could feel that the Cub was ready to fly. Since a good offense is the best defense, I held the wheels of the Cub on the ground and pointed the nose directly at the men in the back of the truck.

Before they could raise their guns to get a shot off at me, they realized that they were only seconds from being chewed to bits by the spinning propeller. Between the early light of dawn and the illumination from the burning barn, I could see the sheer terror on their faces as they dropped their guns and tumbled over one another trying to find safety behind the truck.

During my crop dusting days, I had learned just how close I could come to an obstacle and still be able to pull up and miss it. I held the Cub down until I was no more than fifty feet from the truck before I hauled back on the stick. I was looking eye to eye at the driver as the Cub leaped off the ground and its wheels missed the cab by inches.

The instant that I had cleared the truck, I shoved the nose down and leveled out with the wheels only inches above the grass in order to present the smallest possible target and to gain speed as rapidly as possible in ground effect. There was a row of trees at the end of the runway so I pulled up at the last instant, roared over them and dropped back to ground level behind them. If the men with the guns couldn't see me, there was a very good chance that they couldn't hit me.

It was now light enough that I could see that it was still overcast but the clouds had lifted considerably and there was two or three miles of visibility. When I felt that I was well out of range of their guns, I pulled up to a few hundred feet of altitude and swung the nose toward the eastern sky which was just taking on a rosy hue. I looked back just in time to see the barn tumble into a heap of burning rubble, sending a plume of sparks into the air. A column of smoke rose straight up from the fire and disappeared into the low clouds. I fastened my seatbelt and checked the engine gauges. Everything was normal and the engine was running smoothly. I leaned out the open door and sniffed the air coming off the engine. It smelled normal and I could see no signs of damage other than the hole in the side window. The controls moved easily which indicated that a lucky shot hadn't hit anything critical.

CHAPTER FIFTEEN

I pulled the Nebraska road map out of the pocket in the back of the front seat and opened it to see if I could determine exactly where the town called Sanger was located. I was surprised to find how many miles it was north of my intended route and planned fuel stop at Omaha. If I continued my present heading, it would take me to Sioux City, Iowa which was more along the route to Oshkosh.

I hadn't kept a record on the amount of fuel I burned out of the wing tank before I landed at Sanger and hadn't checked it before takeoff, so I had no idea how much fuel remained in that tank. The only certain amount of fuel that I had aboard was the main tank which was full. I decided to switch back to the wing tank and run on it until it ran out before switching back to the nose tank. That way I would know that I had nearly twelve gallons of fuel remaining which would provide almost three hours flying time, enough to take me several miles away from Sanger and toward my destination.

It finally dawned on me that if I had slipped back in time to 1946, then why was I still thinking about going to Oshkosh. I wouldn't be due there for forty years. My first instinct was to reverse course and return to Colorado, but that would also be back in the direction of Sanger where the sheriff and his drunken mob of vigilantes were waiting for me. I wanted to get as far away from them as possible before I had to land for fuel. Also, if it was 1946 everywhere, then the home that I had built in Colorado wouldn't exist. In fact, the town of Black Forest where I lived didn't even exist in 1946.

My next thought was to turn toward Texas where I had lived in 1946, but what would I do when I got there. Evidently, it was also 1946 there because the operator had obtained the telephone number of my parents. She would probably tell the sheriff that I had tried to call someone with the same name as mine and that would be the first place that the police would look for me. The other thing which really bothered me was that if I was now 57 years old, then did I also exist someplace as a 17 year old.

I finally decided that the best thing for me to do at this point was to continue on course as originally planned and try to decide my best course of action. Considering all the problems that the difference in money had caused in Sanger, I was certainly going to have to be careful in order to keep the same thing from happening again. I might not be lucky enough to escape the next time. Sitting in some federal prison as a counterfeiter would be a terrible way to spend the rest of my life.

I had no idea how I was going to go about buying gasoline once that I got to Sioux City since trying to spend 1986 style money would probably bring the police down on me again. I had credit cards for all of the major suppliers of aviation fuel, and since they were clearly marked with the brand names, I might be able to convince the airport operator that credit cards were something new and get him to sell me fuel on credit. One thing for sure, I wasn't going to be able to fly around forever while trying to decide what to do, so I swung the nose of the Cub a bit to the left and settled back in the seat.

The eastern sky slowly turned to a rosy pink and suddenly a thin slice of the sun stabbed between the earth and the overcast. As I flew on, the band of blue grew wider and for a brief period of time, the sun appeared as a red ball sandwiched between the ground and the clouds. I could feel the warmth of the sun on my face just before it moved behind the cloud deck. A few miles further, I looked up through the skylight to see a patch of blue through a hole in the clouds above me. I was coming to the edge of the overcast. I pulled out the map and began to climb higher in order to make locating my position easier.

From about two thousand feet above the ground I could see several small towns scattered out in front of me and I tried to relate them to the towns on the road map. The main problem associated with flying across the central plains is the fact that most of the rural towns are all the same size and all look alike from the air. The problem is further complicated by the fact that nearly all of the roads are laid out either north and south or east and west. Ground features aren't shown on most road maps whereas aviation charts will show many of the references such as small streams and lakes, making pilotage much easier. It took about half an hour of checking the various towns against the map before I felt sure of my position. I had passed Norfolk off to the right which put me about forty miles from Sioux City. I corrected my course slightly for a direct route there and within about fifteen minutes, I began to see the outline of the Missouri River and then a large city ahead.

From a distance, all cities look the same. There will be a tight group of tall buildings which indicate the core of the city and then they slope off toward the outer edge of town. Off to one side, usually near a river, will be the rusty industrial area belching smoke and haze. Trees are a good indication of the social and economic status of certain parts of the town, with the largest trees located in the most affluent locations. Newly developed areas will appear as stark as strip mines in Appalachia. Tentacles of urban growth follow the main highways as they stretch out from the body.

I could make out the tree lined banks of the Missouri River as it meandered toward St. Louis and its juncture with the great Mississippi. I began to search for an airport as soon as I was close enough to be able to make out details such as highways and railroads. With the sun now up, rotating beacons would have been turned off but it is usually easy to spot runways and hangars because they have a very distinctive shape and size.

The road map indicated an airport south of town and just east of the river so I began to look for the usual signs. I wondered if it was there in 1946. When I was about ten miles away, I could see that a long line of the town extended along the highway so I began to descend slowly and look for signs of an airport.

When I was about a thousand feet above the ground, I spotted a speck in the sky which turned into an airplane which seemed to be climbing as it headed westward. By retracing his angle of climb back to the ground, I was able to pick out a long open space with what appeared to be a number of large buildings along the side nearest the highway. This was the unmistakable signs of an airport. As I came closer, I could see a paved runway as well as a number of airplanes on the ramp. I looked along both sides of the runway for a control tower as the last thing that I would want to do is come puttering across the middle of a controlled airport. I had completely forgotten all about having a radio in my back pack. Seeing no sign of a tower, I changed my heading slightly in order to bring me across the middle of the field where I would be able to see the wind sock and be in a position to enter downwind for whichever runway was being used.

The wind sock was hanging limp and since there was no wind, I would land on the runway from which the other airplane seemed to have come and was also closest the main offices of the airport. I scanned the traffic pattern for other airplanes and seeing none, pulled the carburetor heat on and turned into the downwind leg of a landing pattern. Just after I passed the end of the runway, I turned base and checked to be sure that there was no airplane on a long final approach, burped the engine and banked into a short final.

I glided over the huge numbers 17 painted on the end of the runway, eased the nose up and let the fat tires scrunch against the pavement. I turned off the runway at the first intersection and began to taxi past a long line of parked airplanes. It was only then that I realized that I was passing nothing but airplanes with nose wheels, then I spotted a Piper Navajo, an airplane which wasn't built until well into the 1970s. I was back in 1986! A man stepped from a building with a Shell sign and directed me to an empty tiedown space.

"Fill both tanks with 87 if you have it and Aero Shell 30 in a red can if it needs any oil," I told the line boy as he pulled tiedown ropes through the rings at the outer ends of the lift struts. I got my shaving kit out of my backpack and headed for the terminal building. When I emerged from the rest room, I was washed, shaved, combed and feeling much better about life.

"Is there a restaurant on the field?" I asked the lady behind the counter.

"No, but there is a Ho Jo right across the street," she answered.

Even though I had been awake all night and should have been dog tired; a good breakfast, several cups of hot coffee plus an over-supply of adrenalin from the excitement of the previous night had me ready for the eight hours of flying which still lay between me and Oshkosh. During that long day of puttering across the nation's corn belt, I had ample time to reflect on what had taken place in that little town in Nebraska.

I decided that when I handed the ship over to John, I would simply tell him that the hole in the window had come from a stray bullet while the ship was tied down, avoiding any attempt to explain what had really happened. I still wasn't totally sure if all of those things really did take place or if it was just a very bad dream. If it was simply a dream, it was the most vivid one that I'd ever experienced.

CHAPTER SIXTEEN

Two years had passed since that fateful night in Sanger but the memories of it still haunted me. Memories of that night didn't come to me very often during the day, but those frightening hours kept creeping into my dreams when I was asleep. At times, it would be for only a few fleeting moments, but on other occasions those dreams became as vivid and real as it had been when it was happening all over again. Often, I would be jolted from a deep sleep to find myself gasping for breath and covered with sweat.

The worst problem was the fact that I still wasn't certain whether those memories were real or just products of my mind. There seemed to be no way to make the dreams go away and I knew that one day I would have to return to Sanger if I was to ever know any peace of mind. At one point, I even considered seeking professional help but doing so would force me to admit that there was possibly something wrong with my mind. The only solution was to return to Sanger and see for myself if it was true.

I needed to make a trip back east and would normally have taken Interstate 70 in order to avoid the congestion found along interstate 80 between Chicago and Cleveland. No matter how much I might have wanted to avoid the congestion, I had to take the northern route through Nebraska so I could return to Sanger. There are certain things which a person must do and this was one of them for me.

Even while rolling through the lush farmland around Kearney, I was still having my doubts as to the wisdom of going anywhere near that town. What would I find there? Would there be a warrant for my arrest for breaking out of jail? Would it be 1988 there or would the place still be stuck 40 years behind the rest of the world? Questions, questions, questions, but no answers came to me as I drove along the Interstate. When I came to the exit which would take me to Sanger, I pulled off but it took me several minutes before I could make up my mind whether to make the turn left or pull back onto the Interstate and go about my business. No matter how many times I asked the question, the answer was always the same: I had to go.

I began to look for the airport as I approached Sanger from the east but it was no longer there. The area where the runway had been was covered by tall green corn. The only indication that there had been an airport there was the pole with the metal frame that held the wind sock and the old metal hangar where I had parked the Cub. The outriggers for the door tracks were still there but the doors were missing. A couple tractors were parked inside of it. The other hangar, the office building and all other signs of what it had been were all gone. The roof was gone from the deserted farm house next to the airport and what was left of the walls was leaning askew, appearing ready to tumble into a pile of old lumber. I could see no evidence of where the barn had been. It had obviously burned completely to the ground and weeds had grown up to hide the ashes.

A huge white grain elevator now stood in the space between the road and the railroad tracks where the old elevator and the tractor dealership had once been. It stretched nearly for an eighth of a mile in length and stood hundreds of feet into the air. Wheat crops must have been good over the years as this elevator would hold thousands of times the amount of grain as the old one.

A half dozen pickup trucks were parked around the Dairy Queen which now occupied the spot where the Studebaker place once stood. A sign in the window advertised the Hungerbuster for 99 cents. I parked between two of the pickups, went inside and ordered a cup of coffee. As I sipped the coffee, I listened to the conversation going on among the occupants of two of the booths. They all wore those adjustable baseball caps with advertising printed across the front. Most of them dealt with brands of seeds or John Deere tractors. All that the men seemed to be able to talk about was the weather and how much money the government would cheat them out of this year. One of them said that if the government didn't come through with drought aid soon, it would probably rain and ruin their chances of getting that money. Obviously, the place was now firmly entrenched in the current time period.

Leaving the Dairy Queen, I drove along the main street toward the center of town. I noticed that the building which had been the City Cafe was now a used clothing store called Kathy's Kloset. The bank now has a new stainless steel face covering the old brick front and their drive-in tellers occupy the area across the street where the hotel once stood. The drug store had been completely remodeled and the soda fountain had been replaced with a cosmetics counter. The flashing neon sign advertised that it was one of the Revco chain of stores.

The old water tower bearing the name of the town was gone, replaced by a new one which looks like a giant golf ball on a tee. It was snow white and didn't even have the town's name on it. I parked in front of the courthouse and sat there for a considerable length of time, debating whether I should go in or use my better judgment and drive away. The sheriff, if he is still alive, would have to be at least ninety years old by now and probably can't remember the time of day, much less something that happened over forty years ago.

The courthouse hadn't changed a bit from the way that I remembered it. Still an ugly building with the odd spelling of all words which contained the letter U. The statue of liberty still guarded the right side of the sidewalk and the cannon the other. The only changes that I could see was that Miss Liberty was now missing her arm and a piece of steel rebar had been welded across the muzzle to prevent anyone from shoving something down the barrel.

I'd come this far, so I might as well plunge on. I walked up the front steps, between the Gothic columns and pulled on the brass handle on the huge oak door. My footsteps echoed as I walked across the tiled floor. I knew that the room in the basement where I had been held was nothing more than a holding cell and that the sheriff's office was located elsewhere in the building, probably on the third floor with the jail.

I looked around for a directory of the offices and finding none, stepped into the County Clerk's office which happened to be the one nearest the door. There was only one person in the office, a lady who was pecking away at a computer terminal. Several huge books were was lying on a table with a green top.

"Pardon me, could you tell me where the sheriff's office is located?" I asked.

She looked up, smiled and answered, "In the new building across the street." She pointed toward the back of the courthouse and returned her attention to the computer screen.

I was surprised to find that the road machinery which had been parked behind the courthouse was gone, the chain link fence was missing and the area was now paved for a parking lot. Across the street stood a squat, gray brick building with a small sign which identified it as the Hulsey County Sheriff's Department.

The reception area was clean and smelled of new paint. Immediately to the left of the entrance was a gray steel door with a window less than a foot square. The glass in the window was the type with chicken wire in it. Above the door was a sign stating that visiting hours for the jail were between 2:00 and 4:00 PM on Mondays and Thursdays and that all packages and handbags would be searched. Three more doors opened into the reception area. A young lady dressed in a khaki uniform and wearing a badge was working at a computer terminal behind a glass partition. There were two telephones on the desk and a stack of two-way radios against the wall.

"May I see the sheriff?" I asked the lady.

She picked up one of the phones, pressed a button and I heard the sound of a buzzer come from behind one of the office doors. "Someone here to see you, Sheriff Nester," she said.

She listened for a second, hung up the phone, pointed and said, "Last door on the left."

Sheriff Nester! What was this, Groundhog Day all over again? Was this one of those days that you lived over and over again and could not escape? Was this the short, red haired Sheriff that came so close to getting me killed?

I wasn't sure why I was doing this and what I was going to say to the sheriff, but since I had come this far, there was no backing out now. My heart was in my throat as I walked to the door which opened before I could knock or reach for the knob.

"I'm Sheriff Nester," said a man who appeared to be around forty years of age as he held out his hand. He was dressed in a neat business suit and looked nothing like what I had expected. He wasn't wearing a badge and if he was carrying a pistol under his coat, it wasn't obvious. I suppose that I had prejudged him to be more or less like the other sheriff.

"Thanks for seeing me. My name is Jim Foreman," I replied and instantly wished that I had given him some other name.

I couldn't be sure if it was only my anticipation or if he reacted to the mention of my name. He smiled, invited me in, closed the door and motioned me to one of the two leather chairs in front of his desk.

"What can I do for you Mr. Foreman?"

I didn't want to plunge right into my questions about something which might have happened before he was even born. In fact, I still wasn't sure whether I should approach the subject or not. After all, he was the sheriff and there might still be a warrant for my arrest laying around in his files. I had no idea what the statue of limitations would be on escaping from jail or if there even was one. I wished that I had contacted a lawyer before I came here and had him determine what the situation was. He clasped his hands behind his head, leaned back in his chair and studied me carefully. It was obvious that since he had asked what he could do for me, he was waiting for me to say something.

"I seem to remember that the man who was sheriff here back in 1946 had the same name as yours. Are you any relation?"

"No, we just happen to have the same last name," he replied.

He didn't volunteer any more information and it was obvious that if I was going to learn anything, I would have to make the first move. The only problem was that I really had no idea of how to go about asking him to tell me about something which had happened more than 40 years ago. I decided to stick with questions which were relatively safe in nature.

"Have you lived here in Sanger very long?"

"Yes, all of my life," he replied.

This was getting me nowhere. He wasn't cutting me an inch of slack. It seemed that he was simply waiting for me to ask the wrong question or make a statement which he could use against me. I almost expected him to read me my Miranda warning that I had the right to remain silent. Since it would be impossible for me to remain silent at this point, perhaps the best thing for me to do would be to ask if he knew someone whom I was sure that had never been around Sanger and then get out of this place.

"I'm looking for a man by the name of Robert Benson," I said, using the name of my cousin. "He is supposed to live somewhere in this area and I wondered if you knew him."

"No, I don't believe that I know a Robert Benson, but I know who you are Mr. Foreman, and probably why you are here."

"How could you know me. I haven't been in this town but once in my life and that was many years ago," I replied, in a state of mind which alternated between shock and panic.

"I know all about you and knew that one day you would come back here. I was just waiting for the day when you did."

He turned to a file cabinet, opened the bottom drawer and fingered through several folders before he found the one he wanted. He removed a photograph from the folder and held it up for me to see. It was a black and white photo of me holding a chalkboard with my name on it! It was the photo taken when I was here before.

"I knew who you were the second that you walked through the door," he said as he leafed through the other items in the folder. He opened a small white envelope and dumped five quarters on his desk. Then he pulled out a wrinkled and tattered warrant which showed signs that it had been handled many times. It had my name on it.

"Does this mean that you are going to arrest me?" I asked.

"Heavens no," he said with a laugh. "This thing was issued more than forty years ago and while it might still be legally valid, I would be the last person in the world to serve it on you. Besides that, I know that there was no basis for your original arrest."

"That's certainly a load off my mind. I was afraid for a moment that I was going to be back in jail and from the looks of things, it might be a lot harder to escape this time."

"I've just been playing a cat and mouse game with you and I apologize. Now what did you really want to know."

"Well, the first thing that I wanted to be sure of is whether I had really had been here or if it was just a bad dream. It would appear that I actually traveled back through time and spent a very tense night here in 1946."

"From what I have heard and read about it, you were lucky to have escaped," he said.

"What ever happened to that sheriff?"

"He kept telling the story about having captured a man from a flying saucer and sent warrants to Colorado and Texas. There is also a letter in the file from Sheriff Anderson in Texas that he wrote when he returned the warrant. He said that he knew you and since you were only 18 years old, you couldn't be the person who was wanted here."

"I knew Sheriff Anderson, but he never said anything about a warrant from here," I replied.

"The sheriff kept telling that wild story and searching for you until everyone figured that he had really gone off the deep end. Shortly after that, he and several of his so-called special deputies were indicted and tried for killing a prisoner. They were all convicted and sent to the penitentiary. The sheriff was stabbed to death by another inmate less than a month after he got there. It seems that an ex-sheriff doesn't live very long in prison."

"There was a deputy by the name of Melvin. He tried to help me escape. What ever happened to him?"

"Melvin Simpson is another story. No one is sure how he made his money, but he is without a doubt the richest man in town. He owns the grain elevator, the bank and about half of the farms in the county. He was the other Sheriff Nester's nephew."

"While I was here, I met a lady who had been married to the sheriff at one time. Her name was Maggie. Did you happen to know her?"

"Yes, you might say that I knew Maggie very well. She lived here until she died about ten years ago. She was my mother and a few years before she died, she told me all about you. You see, the reason I know so much about you is because I was born on May 21st, 1947. You are my father."

FOLLOWING MY DREAM

When I lived in Colorado I bought a nice J-3 Cub, not a show quality restoration but no dog. I attempted to set a world altitude record for a 3 liter normally aspirated gasoline engine but missed it by about 400 feet. Got to 31,800 which actually beat the old record but not by the 3% that the FAI required for a new record.

Then I got the idea that a flight with a landing in all 48 contiguous states with camping most of the way would be a neat way to gather photos and stories for a book. It would be done strictly VFR and no electronic navigation. Even though I'd take along a 720 channel hand held, I wouldn't land at any controlled airports. I'd owned it for the better part of a year and flown it some 50 hours without a hint of trouble.

It was coming up on time for an annual and with less than 100 hours on the engine since major, there was nothing needed on it. However I did overhaul the mags and carburetor plus new wires and plugs. Also a new set of tires.

I kissed my wife goodbye and set out on my odyssey shortly after noon on May 1, 1985. My first planned stop was the highest airport in the US; Leadville, Colorado, elevation 9927 feet. The listed service ceiling on the Cub is 11,500, but the balmy 60° day shoved the density altitude to over 12,500 feet. By working thermals and some ridge lift, I finally squeaked in with perhaps a hundred feet to spare.

Good judgment would have dictated that I get to a lower altitude but fun and prudence don't always go together so I pitched my tent in the trees behind the office, had a good dinner at the Golden Burro in town and was in bed as soon as it was dark. Altitude is also highly conducive to sleeping I was soon snuggled in my sleeping bag.

I was awakened at a few minutes past midnight by the sound of rain falling on the tent and the realization that the 20° rating on my sleeping bag was a bit optimistic. I put my clothes on but what body heat there might have been inside the bag had escaped and I shivered in misery the rest of the night. When I finally heard car door slam at the office, I was out of there in search of hot coffee.

The right wing of the Cub drooped, the right tire was flat. I borrowed a car to go into town while the sun had a chance to work on the layer of ice coating everything. I used their air tank to inflate the tire but could hear the air leaking out so it had to come off. One of the beauties of the fat, donut tires on a Cub is they can be serviced without pulling the wheels. All one really needs is a screw driver, knife blade or even a nail to flip the lock ring off so the tire and tube can be pulled as a unit.

A casual inspection of the tubes had indicated that they were in good shape when I put them in the new tires but a closer looks showed age cracks around the valve stem, about the only place where one of those tubes can't be patched.

Now one doesn't walk into a Western Auto Store and ask for a pair of 8.00 x 4 tubes, they never heard of that size and the fact that they haven't been used on any production airplane in about 20 years made them even harder to find. Half a dozen phone calls later and two of them were on their way from California to the tune of nearly fifty bucks each plus a hefty shipping fee to get them there in two days.

Based on my experience in the tent the night before, I decided that a hotel room was in order. One day in Leadville can be sort of fun but the next one gets to be a drag. Two days turned into three before the brown truck dropped the box off for me. In the meantime, my sinuses had plugged up like a toilet in a Pemex station in Mexico. With the new tubes installed, I bought a miserly four gallons of gas to keep the weight down and put the ship in a hangar so it would be ice-free the next morning.

The outside thermometer stood at 24° when I got there the next morning, which happens to be standard temperature at that altitude. At least I had no density altitude to contend with. I thought the oil temperature would never come off the peg and then I used nearly all the mile of runway to get it in the air.

With all the problems I had getting it to 10,000 feet, there was no way I was about to head north where some of the passes were well over 11,000 feet. I followed the road down the valley to Buena Vista and turned east, retracing the route I'd flown to get there. I'd have to get east of the front range before turning north.

The mountains slid behind me as the Front Range of the Rockies fell away with Castle Rock standing like a fortress belome. To the north was the Denver TCA and to the south was Black Forest and the home I'd left four days before.

My sinuses were plugged to where I could barely breathe and my head pounded like a drum. It was decision time, left to follow my dream to right to my home. I thought about it for a few minutes and concluded that I couldn't give up after only five days so I swung the nose to the left after I'd passed the Centennial Airport Control Zone and dropped down to get under the 30 mile outer ring of the TSA inverted wedding cake. At 500 feet AGL, I could slip under the TSA and get into the Aurora Airport. The coat hanger fuel gauge was bumping bottom as I turned final at Aurora. True to the fuel gauge, I had 30 minutes left as put in 10.5 gallons.

Flew east a few miles from Aurora to where I could turn north and past the east end of the runways of the new Front Range Airport. Acres and acres of concrete but no airplanes, just construction machinery.

I'd been in the air for a little over an hour by the time I came to Greeley, where I'd top the tank for the two hour jump to my next destination of Scottsbluff, Nebraska. It's also a 120 miles with few checkpoints. One hour to the first checkpoint at Pine Bluffs on I-80 which I hit right on the nose and another hour to Scottsbluff. I now had three states in my logbook and after five hours in the air, I felt like crap and was ready to call it quits for the day. I had them put the Cub in a hangar and caught a ride into town.

As I checked into a hotel, I asked if there was a doctor around. The guy at the desk suggested my best bet would be the emergency room at the hospital so I caught a cab there. The lady doc looked down my throat, took my temperature, wrote me a prescription for some antibiotics and told me to get a good night's rest and take all the pills.

I felt quite a bit better the next morning and was off on the two hour flight to Hot Springs, South Dakota where I'd check off another state. As I touched down, there was a loud scraping sound coming from the rear and I had no steering on the tailwheel. The flat spring had snapped off right where the bolt holding the tailwheel to it went through and the wheel was flopping around secured only by the two springs. A closer inspection showed that it had been broken on one side for some time. The crack was hidden under the tailwheel bracket and couldn't be seen unless the tailwheel was removed.

There was no mechanic at the field but the guy running the gas pump said he knew someone who might be able to fix it. I took the spring off and used the courtesy car to drive into the small town where I found the guy in a barn full of all sorts of machinery and junk. A partially restored Ford Model T sat on sawhorses just inside the door. He looked at the broken spring for a bit then began to dig through piles of what appeared to be junk. He'd pick up something, look at it and toss it aside. Finally he dragged out the seat off a buggy or buckboard with the double springs under each end of it. They happened to be the same width and thickness as the broken tailwheel spring so after a bit of pounding with a big hammer and chisel, he had one of them free.

He fired up an old fashioned forge like you see in blacksmith shops in western movies. He said my job was to crank the blower when he told me to. After heating the spring to a glowing red color, followed by a lot of beating and banging on an anvil, he had a section cut out of the spring matching the broken one. He drilled the necessary hole in each end then heated it to a cheery red again before plunging it into a barrel of water where it sent up a cloud of steam.

"You gotta soften spring steel to where you can work it and then anneal it so it will be a spring again," he explained to me.

"What do I owe you?" I asked when he handed me the spring.

"How does five bucks sound?" he asked.

"Sounds like a bargain at twice the price," I replied.

The day was shot by the time I got the tailwheel back on using tools borrowed from the cropduster/airport manager. I tied the Cub down and since I didn't feel like a night in a tent, I caught a ride to a hotel in town. Following dinner, I soaked for a while in the mineral hot springs from which the place got its name. That seemed to improve my disposition if not my sore throat.

From Hot Springs it was an hour to Newcastle, Wyoming where I'd need to top the tank for the long hop to Sheridan, Wyoming. By the time I landed at Sheridan, my throat was afire and I could barely talk. To add to my woes, as I applied the brakes when turning off the runway, the right brake pedal sagged to the stop. I talked with the mechanic who said he'd put it in the shop and look at it later. I caught a cab straight to the VA hospital where I figured that since I had no insurance and was a veteran, I could get treated at no cost.

I discovered that while getting into a VA Hospital is difficult, getting out can be a bigger problem. After endless forms to fill out and telephone calls to verify that I was both who I claimed and that I was indeed a veteran, they finally sent me to be examined. It was no quick look down my throat, take my temperature which they said was 102°, but poke and prod me from end to end, draw blood and had me pee in a cup. Then they trundled me off to a room where a nurse woke me up every hour to bother me some more. The next morning the doctor told me I had a serious case of Strep Throat caused by a virus and since I wasn't contagious they were moving me to a ward. I asked him how long I would be there. He said it would take a week with no treatment or seven days with it but they could make me a lot more comfortable while I was there. He added that I shouldn't be driving and when he learned that I was flying, he said that I definitely shouldn't be doing any of that.

I called my wife to tell her where I was and not to worry because I was in no danger and in good hands. Four days and a bunch of pills later I was feeling much better but having trouble sleeping in the ward with nurses coming in to check me every hour and all the people snoring, coughing and gagging. They signed me out the next day at noon so I checked with the mechanic. He said the expansion tube in the right brake was leaking and he hadn't ordered any parts. I told him to put the wheel back on and I'd fly it that way.

Then I got a hotel room, had a good dinner and slept like a log all night. Since I was two grand and two weeks into the flight, camped only one night and visited only three states, the trip wasn't turning out anything like I had envisioned, I pointed the nose south the next morning and was home that night. Should I ever decide to pursue that dream again, I have only 44 states left.

This proves that following your dream can turn into a nightmare.

5483607R00102

Made in the USA
San Bernardino, CA
09 November 2013